My Vampire vs Your Werewolf

Paul Tobin

BLOOMSBURY
CHILDREN'S BOOKS
NEW YORK LONDON OXFORD NEW DELHI SYDNEY

BLOOMSBURY CHILDREN'S BOOKS
Bloomsbury Publishing Inc., part of Bloomsbury Publishing Plc
1385 Broadway, New York, NY 10018

BLOOMSBURY, BLOOMSBURY CHILDREN'S BOOKS, and the Diana logo
are trademarks of Bloomsbury Publishing Plc

First published in the United States of America in September 2024
by Bloomsbury Children's Books

Text copyright © 2024 by Paul Tobin

All rights reserved. No part of this publication may be reproduced or transmitted in any form
or by any means, electronic or mechanical, including photocopying, recording, or any
information storage or retrieval system, without prior permission in writing from the publisher.

Bloomsbury books may be purchased for business or promotional use.
For information on bulk purchases please contact Macmillan Corporate and
Premium Sales Department at specialmarkets@macmillan.com

Library of Congress Cataloging-in-Publication Data
Names: Tobin, Paul, author.
Title: My vampire vs. your werewolf / by Paul Tobin.
Other titles: My vampire versus your werewolf
Description: New York : Bloomsbury Children's Books, 2024.
Summary: In a friendly competition sanctioned by the Crafters Guild to
combat monster mental health, nine-year-old trainers Gabe and Hayden bring
two exiled monsters to compete in a no-holds-barred fight.
Identifiers: LCCN 2024015793 (print) | LCCN 2024015794 (e-book)
ISBN 978-1-61963-901-0 (hardcover) • ISBN 978-1-5476-1564-3 (paperback)
ISBN 978-1-61963-902-7 (ePub)
Subjects: CYAC: Monsters—Fiction. | Contests—Fiction. | Mental health—Fiction. |
Horror stories. | LCGFT: Monster fiction. | Horror fiction. | Novels.
Classification: LCC PZ7.1.T6 My 2024 (print) | LCC PZ7.1.T6 (e-book) | DDC [Fic]—dc23
LC record available at https://lccn.loc.gov/2024015793

Book design by Yelena Safronova
Typeset by Westchester Publishing Services
Printed and bound in the U.S.A.
2 4 6 8 10 9 7 5 3 1

To find out more about our authors and books
visit www.bloomsbury.com and sign up for our newsletters.

This book goes out to my four most important life mentors: My mom and dad. My wife, Colleen. And Red, the dog I had when I was a teenager.

My Vampire vs Your Werewolf

CHAPTER 1

Gabe hammered his chisel into the ancient stone seal on the dust-covered doorway. He felt like one of those archaeologists who unearths lost tombs and discovers treasures hidden for centuries. What he was doing was far different, though. He and his partner, Hayden, were outside Wrexham in Wales, working in the murky darkness of a dungeon beneath an ancient castle abandoned centuries in the past. And they weren't looking for treasure. Far from it. They were searching for a vampire.

"Count Drustan," Hayden whispered. "He's here. Beyond this door. I know it."

Gabe looked to his friend. Like him, she was nine years old. She had long brunette hair, as opposed to his own wiry black hair. Her skin was a pale white, while his was dark. They both had brown eyes, hers glinting in the sparse light from the oil lamps set into the walls of old brick and raw stone.

Gabe stopped working for a moment, tired from all the hammering. He'd been chiseling away for what felt like forever—whoever sealed up this doorway *really* didn't want people getting in. The doorway had been blocked off hundreds of years before to forbid access to the room beyond, where—as legend had it—a vampire had been trapped in his own castle. The seal on the doorway was of a dark red marble with delicate white veins, carved with a wolf's head in relief. Gabe's chisel had scoured away most of the wolf, sending splinters of stone to collect in the dust at his feet. The seal, according to Hayden's research, was magic. A spell of protection. Until the seal was destroyed, the wall would remain invulnerable.

The dungeon's depths were lost to shadows, impervious to the oil lamps hanging from the walls or even the flashlight Hayden carried. Now and then she thought she saw eyes in the darkness, or the blackest of shadows slinking away from the light. The arched doorway she and Gabe were facing had been blocked by a wall of dense rocks held together with a powerful mortar, along with the impressive stone seal. It was all that stood between them and the vampire they were searching for. And Hayden was getting anxious.

Gabe flexed his fingers. Chiseling was hard work. Unclipping his own flashlight from his belt, he studied the dungeon, the rows of prison cells with their rusty iron bars and their manacles chained to the walls. A slow tide of rainwater seeped down the stairs, and maybe it was just the dirt and grime or a trick of the light, but Gabe swore it looked like blood.

"This place is creepy," he told Hayden.

"I bet it was nice once, though," she said. "Well, maybe not down here in the dungeon, but up there." She shined her flashlight toward the ceiling. Something large scuttled away into the darkness. Maybe the castle had been magnificent, once, long ago in its vampire overlord's day, but no longer. On their trek to the dungeon, creeping through the castle, they'd been forced to squeeze past huge wooden doors—half devoured by termites—slumped against cracked iron hinges. Together, their boots had stirred up thick clouds of dust and crunched through the untold layers of beetle shells littering the floors like a fallen army, adding to the castle's cloying scents of iron, stone, and decay. They'd encountered endless piles of dust-covered bones tucked into corners. The majority had been animal bones, but a few of the skeletons had been human, clad in moldy remnants of clothing and bearing rings on their bony yellow fingers.

Water trickled down several walls and dripped from above, building into tiny rivulets that acted as reminders of the storm raging outside, the one that had given them no pause when they'd scrambled out of their hired car to take in the castle outlined before them in the darkness, a presence so immense that Gabe had almost balked. But the storm left them no choice but to clamber over toppled walls into the castle's forsaken depths.

They'd crept through the forbidden halls while following a map derived from Hayden's research, passing fallen tapestries that had become nests for rats, with their glinting eyes peeking out from the musty, decaying folds. The cramped dungeon stairway had been almost entirely blocked by a monstrous network of spiderwebs that felt like dry fingers grabbing at them, pulling them back. Gabe could still feel spiders crawling along his arms and all through his hair, and as he stood in the shadows cast from the flickering oil lamps, he saw Hayden puffing a breath to blow away a fat arachnid crawling across her cheek.

"Do you think he's really in here?" Gabe asked.

"Absolutely," Hayden said, wiping dust and sweat from her brow, studying the stone wall that barred access to the final chamber. It was exactly as described in her research findings, built from heavy gray stones worked into a nearly flat plane, with warnings of what waited beyond etched into their surface.

"Vampire," the words read, again and again. "Vampire. Beware." Hayden ran her fingers over the words, then gave an involuntary yelp when Gabe resumed work, with his chisel biting deep into the seal, sending a shock wave through the stones and into her fingers, as if she'd been bitten. Mortar crumbled from around the seal.

"Count Drustan," Hayden whispered, staring eagerly at the seal. Soon, it would be broken and the chamber beyond could be reached. The chamber. And the coffin. And Count Drustan. The vampire.

The echoes of Gabe's chiseling kept building in the dungeon like a pressure in the air, squeezing at Hayden's chest. And then a sharp *crack*, like the lightning and thunder outside, except this time the sound was that of stone. The seal had broken. A fissure ran through it. The oil lamps fluttered, as if blown by a breeze. Then three of them were snuffed out entirely, allowing the shadows to creep even closer.

"You broke it?" Hayden asked Gabe, who stepped back to assess his work.

"Yeah," he said. "Won't be long, now."

"Good," Hayden said, but she wasn't entirely certain it *was* good. This meant . . . they were minutes from meeting a vampire.

Gabe worked the chisel's tip into the crack he'd caused, and the ringing sounds of his hammer filled the dungeon again. This time the sounds were sharper. The little splinters of marble that had been falling away from the seal now became chunks, hitting the dusty floor with dull thuds or splashing into the murky puddles. And then the entirety of the seal crumbled, with Gabe quickly moving back so that the larger pieces didn't crush his toes.

The atmosphere instantly changed. A tremor rippled through the dust. The shadows began audibly rustling. The heavy stones, blocking access to the chamber beyond, shifted. The mortar that had held them together for centuries began dissolving into a chalky sand, sifting away to the floor. Hayden slid her hand into Gabe's, and, together, they watched the stones collapse, the rumbling noises oddly dulled in the darkness, sounding like an avalanche of snow and ice rather than crushing stone. In seconds it was over, leaving enough space above the rubble that they could clamber over the pile and reach the vampire's chamber. She tightened her grip on Gabe. His hammer fell from his other hand, striking the stone floor with a sharply ringing *clang* that made them both wince.

Hayden took a deep breath and released her friend's hand, then moved forward.

"Might as well do this now," she said, "before I lose my nerve."

The stones shifted beneath her feet, but instead of making it harder to climb over the rubble into the darkness of the newly opened chamber, the stones seemed to be grabbing at her, pulling her inward to the shadows . . . and to the vampire waiting beyond.

CHAPTER 2

Joon Baker checked the time on her phone. It was just after two in the morning in this largely deserted area of Detroit. There were no cars. No pedestrians. No lights in any windows. Nothing stirring except one cat watching from the shadows, and Joon's friend Tradd Risso, who was chaining their bikes to a rusted, badly bent street sign. The streetlight above them barely had the power to illuminate the sidewalk, where they stood in front of a furniture warehouse that had gone out of business ten years ago, about the time Joon and Tradd had been born.

"Not sure we should chain up our bikes," Joon said.

"But they might get stolen," Tradd argued, giving her a look like there wasn't any question that they should chain up their bikes.

"We might need to leave in, uh, a hurry," Joon told him.

He frowned, and then a little jolt of realization shivered through his expression, and his hands—which had been about to click the lock shut—paused.

"Hmm," he said. Tradd was a local, from Detroit. A Caucasian boy with round red glasses and a sweep of dark blond hair so thick that Joon often felt it looked like a ramp. He had a wide nose and flappy ears, and Joon thought he was cute but would never tell him. His large green eyes, normally so playful, now narrowed in concern. *Of course* they might need to leave in a hurry.

They were hunting a werewolf, after all.

"Lock them or not?" Tradd asked, looking to Joon for the final decision. She hesitated. A wrong decision here could be costly. She tried to peer inside the warehouse, looking through a dirty window protected by a rusty iron grille, hoping for—and fearing—a glimpse of the werewolf rumored to live inside, but she saw nothing except her own reflection. A ten-year-old Korean girl. Long brunette hair. Brown eyes. A She-Hulk hoodie. There were no answers there.

"Lock the bikes," Joon told Tradd. "It's true we might need to leave in a hurry, but that won't be possible if someone steals our bikes." Tradd nodded, and Joon heard the sharp *click* of the lock snapping shut. Their bikes would be safe. With that settled, it was now her job to keep herself, and Tradd, safe. The easiest way to do that was to forget this whole thing about tracking down a werewolf and simply leave. But then, obviously, they wouldn't *have* a werewolf. And they needed one.

Joon walked up to a metal fire door and tried the handle. It was locked. No surprise, there. But she'd taught herself how to pick a lock, watching endless hours of online tutorials, practicing around her house and at school and a few other places best kept secret. It only took her two minutes, with Tradd shining his flashlight on the lock.

Click.

The door opened, and the air that rushed out was strangely . . . humid? Holding the door, listening for anything out of the ordinary, Joon peeked inside.

"Huh?" she said. It was nearly a gasp.

"Huh, what?" Tradd asked.

"Huh," Joon repeated, moving back so that Tradd could peer inside, which he did.

"Huh," he said. "You were right."

The inside of the warehouse was one vast space, and it was . . . forested. The entire warehouse was a thick woodland, complete with birds and squirrels and a mechanical moon far above, shining down on the trees below. There was a running stream. Dark pathways of misty soil. It was like some old-growth forest, the type of dense woods where the king's hunters rode through on a fox hunt, or a witch lured children to their doom with a cottage built of candy, or—on certain nights—a werewolf might prowl.

"We're definitely in the right place," Joon said. She moved two steps inside the warehouse, two steps into the humid, waiting forest, with one hand trailing back to touch the doorway, reluctant to leave it behind. Tradd walked past her to run his hand against a tree, feeling the bark.

"It's real," he said. "These trees are real. Why is there a forest inside a warehouse?"

"Because a werewolf lives here," Joon said, moving away from the walls, which were moist and covered in moss. "Let's find him."

Joon and Tradd made their way through the forest. Despite knowing they were inside a warehouse, the woods seemed real, and endless. But of course they were only walking in circles, following paths that forever veered from the walls, keeping the illusion of an infinite forest alive. Some forty feet above, the treetops scratched at the lowest of the ceiling beams and what looked like a train track running through the rafters. Hanging from it was a glowing orb resembling a full moon, moving slowly along the overhead track, casting shadows below.

"This is super spooky," Joon said.

"You're only saying that because you know there's probably a werewolf watching us right now."

"It's a factor," Joon admitted. "Being stalked by a werewolf isn't exactly the way to a girl's heart."

"It's kinda the way to *your* heart, though," Tradd noted,

giving her a grin and then returning to watch the trees and the shadows. Joon had to admit Tradd was right. The times when she was finding monsters were the times she felt the most alive.

The *crack* of a twig snapping came from somewhere behind them. Joon and Tradd went instantly still. They glanced at each other, a silent moment to acknowledge that—yes—they'd both heard the noise. Something was following them. They hurried behind a tree, pressed shoulder to shoulder, peering out from opposite sides back toward where they'd heard the sound. But now the only thing Joon could hear was Tradd's breath, the sounds of the artificial stream echoing through the forest, and the slow churn of the false moon in the rafters above.

"I don't hear anything," Tradd said, nervously adjusting his glasses.

"But we *did* hear something," Joon said. "We can't let our guard down. Werewolves are fast. If we lose focus, he could . . ." Her words ran out. But her eyes said all about what a werewolf could do.

"There has to be a house in here somewhere," Tradd said, gesturing around them. "A hut. Some place where he stays. Probably at the center of this forest. We need to find it."

"There doesn't necessarily *need* to be a house," Joon said. "Werewolves are feral creatures. He could be sleeping on the ground. Or maybe there's a cave?"

"Why would there be a cave in a warehouse?"

"Why would there be a forest in a warehouse?" Joon

asked in reply, rapping her knuckles on the tree they were standing against.

"Good point. Maybe there's—"

Crack.

Another snapping of a twig. But not from where they'd heard the first noise. This one came from behind them again, in the opposite direction. And then . . . *thump* . . . a footfall. Followed by a low drawing of breath, like a sigh from a horse, but more ragged.

"Ah, lemons," Joon hissed, using the worst curse she allowed herself. "Is he behind us?"

"Maybe," Tradd said. By silent agreement, he faced in the direction of this new noise, while Joon remained focused in the direction of the original sound. "It might be smartest if we left."

"Without a doubt," Joon agreed. "But an even smarter thing would be if we never came here in the first place. So, since we're *already* doing stupid things, maybe we should be even stupider?"

"Your logic is . . . not logical."

"Not logical? What are you, Spock? We're werewolf hunters. Not Vulcans. All I'm saying is that if we leave now, we don't get a werewolf, but since we need a werewolf and we're already here, we might as well stay."

"Is this one of your arguments where it's just easier for me to agree?"

"That's *all* of my arguments," Joon said.

"Fair enough," Tradd told her, not adding that he found

it amusing whenever Joon narrowed her eyes, because it made her cute, an observation and opinion that he would take to his grave.

Crack.

Another snapped twig. In a different direction.

"He's doing it on purpose," Joon said, her eyes flickering back and forth as she tried to watch everywhere at once.

"On purpose?"

"A werewolf can be silent in the woods if he wants to be. If he's snapping twigs, it's because he wants us to know he's out there. He wants us to know he's watching. He wants us to know he's stalking us."

"I suddenly know a lot of things that I didn't want to know."

"It's better to know you're being stalked, than to not know, and still be stalked."

"I know," Tradd said. There was movement to the left, maybe twenty feet away. Something flashed into view for a moment, and then was gone.

"We need a wall at our backs," Joon said. "We're too much in the open. We need to cut down his avenues of attack."

"How do you know he's going to attack?" Tradd asked. They were already in motion, but they weren't running. They both knew that blindly running from a werewolf would be a short race with a bloody finish line. Instead of running, they were walking back-to-back, keeping an eye in every direction.

A snarl from one direction. A twig snapping in another. A low, throaty chuckle. A *click-clacking* noise that Tradd couldn't place.

"What's that?" he whispered.

"His jaws," Joon whispered back. "His teeth. Fangs clicking together."

"Ah," Tradd sighed. "More knowledge I didn't really want." They were cutting through the woods, forgoing the trails, with Joon glancing overhead to gauge their position based on the rafters. The warehouse seemed bigger than it had from the outside, which made a certain sense, because outside she'd felt safe, while inside, here in this strange forest, she absolutely wasn't.

Something touched her.

A claw from behind, snagging briefly on the shoulder of her She-Hulk hoodie. Joon gasped and turned quickly, yelling, "Look out!" to warn Tradd, but he was swept to the ground, thumping into the thick soil of the warehouse floor. He grunted with impact, glasses tumbling off into the fallen leaves. Joon whirled, trying to find the werewolf, but he was nothing more than a flash of fur disappearing into the thick trees. Joon quickly helped Tradd to his feet as he hurriedly slid his glasses back into place.

"We need to find a wall," she told him. "And this time we need to *run*." They looked at each other, locking eyes, with a silent countdown in their heads. Three. Two. One.

They ran.

CHAPTER 3

Hayden shined her light on the vampire's coffin. It was made of a dark wood, with hints of a deep red visible through the thick layers of dust. Tearing her gaze away from the vampire's resting place, she looked around the chamber. Other than the rubble-strewn doorway she and Gabe had crawled through, there were no other entrances. No other ways to get out. Despite that, just as it had been in the chamber where they'd broken the seal, oil lamps burned brightly on the walls, with occasional sputtering flares. And, just as they had been outside this chamber with the coffin, these lamps were failing to entirely banish the shadows.

The chamber's walls were carved with warnings. *Vampire. Beware.*

The chamber's floor was carved with warnings. *Beware. Vampire.*

The coffin itself was wrapped with chains, with one final warning on the lock itself. *Don't*, it said. Nothing more.

"They were pretty adamant about keeping Count Drustan locked away," Gabe said. His voice echoed in the chamber, which was roughly the size of a basketball court and possibly twenty feet high, carved from living stone. A miniature waterfall coursed down one wall, no larger than the flow from a kitchen faucet. It ran down over the carved warnings before trickling across the floor along a path where it had obviously flowed for centuries, judging by the channel the water had sliced through the warnings on the floor. The sound was soothing. Melodic. And very out of place in its current setting.

Gabe stood in front of the coffin with its layers of undisturbed dust. Was it even possible that the vampire was still alive inside the coffin, after so many centuries? Well, not exactly *alive*, but . . . whatever word best fit.

Hayden reached out and traced a finger through the coffin's dust. She wrote *vampire*, and *beware*, and then she felt too anxious, so she drew a smiley face with fangs.

"Locked," Gabe said, picking up the lock and the heavy chains. They rumbled and clinked in irritation, disturbed after so many years. Dust slid from the chains as the links uncoiled.

"Good thing we brought the key," Hayden said, swallowing deeply. She reached inside a hidden pocket in her dress and brought out a small glass vial. Filled with blood. From her research, she knew a lock-picking kit wouldn't cut it. This lock had been secured by an ancient magic, much like the seal Gabe had broken on the doorway, and only the blood of a witch could open it. Luckily, they had some friends with connections to a witch, who had been very understanding and happy to help.

Hayden plucked out the cork from the vial and poured the blood into the lock. Immediately the oil lamps flared. The chamber rumbled. The stream momentarily stopped flowing. An abrupt gust of wind—from no source at all—sped through the chamber and swept the dust from the coffin. The heavy lock clicked open. The chains fell away. Gabe reached over and took Hayden's hand. Together, they stepped back.

The coffin began to open.

The slow *creeeeak* of the coffin's lid filled the chamber. Hayden could feel the noise pushing against her, pressing on her skin. It felt like dry fingers. It felt like she should run.

The coffin's lid creaked open another inch. Another. The shadows swirled. Whispers fluttered through the air, like the beating of wings. Gabe felt like he could hear the storm outside, raging against the castle's ancient, crumbling walls. The coffin's lid kept inching upward.

"A hand," Hayden whispered. "I can see his hand." She could barely speak, short of breath. A pale hand was pushing the lid open. Darkness reached outward like tentacles. From somewhere came a wolf's howl, and then low, chuckling laughter.

The coffin's lid sprang open.

And then the vampire was there.

He rose from the coffin, floating upward to stand in mid-air, his eyes glowing red. The vampire was tall, wearing heavy leather boots and finely cut leather pants, with a wrapped tunic of light and dark browns, cinched with a wolf's-head clasp on his wide leather belt. He had a dark brown cloak. Rings with thick gemstones. He had a beard and a mustache, and he smelled like dust and smoke, blood and iron. His skin was emaciated. Withered. He seemed little more than a corpse, except for the fire in his eyes.

"Free," he said. The voice was deep. Hayden felt like it was reaching to her across the centuries.

"Free," the vampire said again, gazing around. Gabe couldn't keep his fingers from trembling. The vampire flickered. Gone to shadows and smoke. He reappeared immediately in front of Gabe and Hayden, only inches away. Gabe felt a shriek rising in his throat, and Hayden gasped, but they both knew what to do. Even as the vampire reached for them, even as the hush of his presence and the chill of his aura swept over them, they held forth the medallions they'd been clutching in their hands.

"Ngh," the vampire grunted. Maybe not a grunt of pain, but at least one of discomfort. The medallions were made of pure gold, about twice the size of a silver dollar, with an image of the sun burning bright.

"Stay back," Gabe told the vampire, holding the medallion, which—like Hayden's—hung from a chain of gleaming gold.

"I am not yours to command," the vampire snarled. He tried to take a step forward, but Gabe and Hayden held firm, shielding themselves with their medallions as the vampire attempted to advance. They could feel his presence in concussive bursts, like the pressure of a tornado coming closer.

"We will not yield, Count Drustan," Hayden said. She tried to put all her bravado and belief into the words. If she and Gabe faltered, the hungry vampire—the *starving* vampire— would be on them.

"You are children," the vampire said. His dry lips curled into a smile, revealing his fangs. Hayden felt whispers in her mind. *Drop the medallion. Throw it into the stream and let it flow away with the water down the fissure in the earth, lost for all time.* Hayden noticed Gabe twitching beside her, obviously struggling with similar whispers in his own mind.

"We are your friends," Hayden said. It took effort to form the words. And even more effort to hold the medallion out in front of her. But she had no other choice. If she failed, she was . . . food.

"Friends?" the vampire scoffed. "The ones who entombed me"—he gestured back to the coffin—"called me their friend. Then, I was betrayed. Sealed within this chamber. But I slept while they died, and I still walk, while they do not." In rage, he reached back and grabbed the coffin, which must have weighed three hundred pounds. He plucked it up with one hand, then hurled it across the chamber to where it shattered on the rocks, bursting into fragments. Before the pieces had landed, the vampire turned into smoke, darting around the room. He turned into a huge raven, and then into a wolf the size of a horse, with slavering jaws snapping shut inches away from Hayden, but she never released her hold on the medallion. She never stepped back.

"We *are* your friends," she said, pronouncing each word slowly, to give them more weight.

"Ridiculous," the vampire said, returning to his human form, with his gaze averted from the medallions. Gabe and Hayden stayed silent, watching the vampire's expressions, trying to guess his thoughts. Count Drustan's heavy brow was furrowed. His lips a thin line. He looked more like a zombie than a vampire, after having gone so long without blood. Several small fragments of the coffin had fallen into the tiny stream and were washed across the floor, building into a passable dam, around which the water was diverting course and seeping across the chamber, lapping at Gabe's feet.

Finally, the vampire let out a long sigh, exhaling centuries-old breath.

"Why are you here, mortals?" Count Drustan asked, a glare in his gaze and his lips pulling back to reveal those fangs.

Gabe and Hayden glanced at each other. This was the moment of truth. If Count Drustan didn't agree to their plans, they would have unleashed this dangerous being for nothing. And not everyone was lucky enough to have a medallion for protection like they did. Gabe nodded at Hayden, and she turned to the vampire once again.

"We need you to fight a werewolf," she said.

"Oh," the vampire replied. His red eyes turned a soothing blue. His snarl dwindled away. The oil lamps flared into stronger life, lighting the dim room and banishing all but the most adamant of shadows. The smell of the water was stronger. The scent of decay vanished.

"Fight a werewolf?" Count Drustan said, beaming a smile. "You should have said so in the first place! That sounds like fun."

CHAPTER 4

The trees flashed past as Tradd and Joon sprinted through the forest. They were aware of little except each other, afraid of being separated. They were also aware of any trees that needed dodging and a small shack they barely glimpsed as they ran past, but mostly they were aware of the werewolf behind them, the snarl of his laughter, the taunting howls, the birds in this misplaced forest gone silent, watching from the safety of the treetops and the rafters above. Leaves whipped across Joon's face as she yelled for Tradd to run faster, both of them stumbling as they hurtled over the stream and landed on softer soil than they'd expected, and then something—a whirling mass of muscle, fur, and teeth—landed in front of them. Joon barely glimpsed the werewolf before she turned to run in another direction, holding Tradd's hand and pulling him along with her, the two of them splashing through the stream in the forest, in the warehouse, with the strange moon shining down from above.

A blur of fur ran past them so fast that Joon could barely comprehend its speed, the water flying up around her, soaking her. Before the water settled, the werewolf was gone. Only the echoes of his mocking laughter remained.

"Keep running!" Joon ordered Tradd, which wasn't strictly necessary, since *he* was the one running ahead now. They'd barely left the stream before one of the trees next to her suddenly sprayed splinters, as if there'd been a small explosion. Joon gasped at the three slashing claw marks in the tree trunk that explained what had just happened.

"Keep running!" she yelled again, to herself as much as to Tradd. Her lungs burned and her legs ached. Then came a deafening howl only inches from her ears, the shock so sudden that she lost her footing and sprawled to the dirt, tangling up with Tradd and rolling into a tree with a painful *smack*. The werewolf flashed past her and leapt an incredible distance up into the tree, then jumped to another tree, and another, bouncing back and forth, shaking their branches as he bounded ever higher until he'd reached the rafters and stood momentarily still, a silhouette of immense power and size standing next to the fake moon on the train track. A howl erupted from his open jaws, sending panicked birds speeding away to the edges of the warehouse as a cascade of leaves fell from all around.

"Lemons," Joon hissed, her entire body sore from her

fall and the impact with the tree, but there was no time to complain, no time to do anything except help Tradd to his feet and then run as fast as they—

The werewolf dropped from above.

A forty-foot drop, but he landed without difficulty, sending dirt billowing in all directions. He'd barely landed before he was moving forward, and then he was standing over Joon.

"Lemons," she said again. Weaker this time.

The werewolf was easily seven feet tall, wearing nothing but torn blue pants. His head was massive, something akin to human, but mostly the head of a wolf. His reddish-gray eyes held intelligence, though the fury of the forest was inside them as well, something primeval that found its joy in the hunt. The werewolf's arms were long, with elongated fingers stretching from extended palms, hair bursting from everywhere, razor claws at the tips of his fingers. His chest was gigantic. Muscles everywhere. A stink like intense garlic. His humid breath washed over Joon as the werewolf panted and chuckled, his body swaying as if there was too much fury to ever be still, too much joy in the hunt to ever stop.

Tradd got to his feet next to Joon.

He held out his medallion.

It was pure silver, with the image of a wolf's head on one side, a "V" on the other. It hung from a tightly linked silver chain.

"Back," Tradd demanded, stepping between Joon and the werewolf. Joon took a moment to admire Tradd's bravery, but she shook her head free of *that*, because she needed her own medallion and she needed it *now*. Her hands searched frantically through the pockets of her hoodie, somehow not finding the medallion's cool metal surface or sleek silver chain. Where *was* it? On their way to the warehouse, and seemingly a hundred times during their walk through the unexpected forest, she'd run her fingers over its smooth, soothing surface, but now it was gone. She *needed* it. One medallion was not enough. A single medallion might stall the werewolf's attack, but not stop it. The werewolf's jaws snapped shut only inches from Tradd's medallion, snarling at it. His claws kept slashing past Tradd's face, cutting the air near his throat. Luckily, the creature couldn't bring itself to get too close to Tradd's medallion. At least, not yet.

"Joon," Tradd said. No more than that. Only her name. She knew what he meant, though. He meant, *Joon, could you please find your medallion? And quickly*? Her fingers searched desperately for her medallion, all through her pockets, but there was nothing. Had it fallen out when she was running? If so, it could be anywhere in the warehouse. Lost in the forest.

High above, a creaking groan came from the small train tracks winding their way through the rafters. The false moon chugged forward a few more inches, casting light in new areas.

From below, in a bed of fallen leaves, a silver glint.

"There!" Joon yelled, and she leapt past the werewolf. His claws slashed through the air, slicing through the back of Joon's hoodie but not—thankfully—her flesh. And then she was rolling with impact, and her aim was perfect, the medallion fitting into her hand as she grabbed it up and rolled into a kneeling position.

"Stay *back*!" she yelled to the beast, holding out her medallion. In reply, the beast howled, his head thrown back and his chest heaving. The howl had a physical presence that Tradd could feel pushing against him, along with a wave of heat. The werewolf was lost in his rage, slashing out to flay open a tree, creating a deep furrow through the bark and wood. His jaws snapped at the air. He howled again and again. Joon felt the heat of his breath and his rage, but kept her fingers clasped tight around her medallion, still holding it out, not letting her fear consume her.

In time, the werewolf stopped slashing at the air. He ceased to howl. His jaws closed. His eyes looked to Joon. Then to her medallion. Then to Tradd and his medallion. The beast's shoulders slumped, then shrugged.

"Oh, whatever," he said. His voice was nearly normal, albeit with an extra quality of rumbling gravel.

"Whatever?" Joon asked. She hadn't expected the werewolf to talk.

"Yeah. Whatever. You got me. Fair's fair." He scratched

his head, then leaned against a tree and regarded Joon and Tradd.

"What do you think of my forest?" he asked. "Pretty cool, right? I'm especially proud of the moon."

CHAPTER 5

Gabe stepped out of the car, thanked the driver, and then closed the door. The car was already pulling away as Gabe brought up his rideshare app and tipped the driver. He put his phone away, standing on the sidewalk in Tacoma, Washington, looking around the neighborhood, which was a mix of small stores and apartment buildings. The late morning sun was peeking above the rooftops.

Leaning against a cherry tree, Gabe nervously dug out his phone again, first checking to see if there were any new texts from Hayden—which there infuriatingly weren't—and then using his camera to see a view of himself and make sure his clothes looked decent and that there wasn't anything stuck in his teeth. Checking the time, he saw he was almost twenty minutes early to the appointment.

"Hmm," he mumbled, again checking for any texts from Hayden, and then walking inside Café Mastodon to order a chocolate donut with orange juice. Sitting at an outside table, he checked his phone again. Four minutes had passed. Still no texts from Hayden. He texted, "I'm here. At the café," and waited for a reply. Nothing. He sent a picture of himself and was composing another text when he realized that the Laws of Texting forbade him from texting so many times in a row, so he set his phone aside and enjoyed his donut, which was thick and chewy with a slab of dark chocolate on top, dappled with sea salt.

"She gets nervous," Gabe muttered to himself, deciding on the probable reason why Hayden was late. She was often anxious around people, and today, they were not only meeting people, but important ones as well. She'd be waiting until the last moment. Hayden was most comfortable in small groups, with people she'd known for a long time. Her friend Mala, for instance. And Ellie and Chen. All three of them teammates on her school's soccer team. Or, give Hayden a library full of books, and she was happy. Or pushing her way into the ruins of ancient castles, where nobody had walked for a hundred years.

Waiting, Gabe watched people walking past. He watched them in their cars, on their bikes, on a couple of scooters, and wondered about their lives. What were they doing? Where were they going? He imagined them looking to *him*, the boy at the café table, and wondering the same things. Could they possibly guess he was waiting for his friend so that they could meet with the Wardens and register their vampire for battle?

Probably not.

Definitely not.

A trio of pigeons milled at his feet. Gabe told them that they couldn't have any of his donut. They didn't take this news well. In fact they didn't take it at all. They simply didn't understand. They undoubtedly couldn't comprehend a werewolf, either. Which, Gabe decided, was fair. He couldn't, either. He wondered how Count Drustan—currently staying a little over a hundred miles away in a cabin on the shore of Lake Chelan—would fare in battle against the werewolf. The vampire was unthinkably fast. And strong. He could turn into a bat or a raven. A wolf. Into nothing more than smoke. Gabe was confident Drustan would have little problem against a werewolf, although he acknowledged he'd never met such a beast.

"Orange juice?" Gabe heard, and looked up to find Hayden standing next to him. She was in a light green dress with leggings. A black barrette in her hair and a dark green shoulder bag with a tattered Frankenstein sticker completed her look.

"What's wrong with orange juice?" Gabe asked. There'd been an accusation in Hayden's tone.

"Nothing," she said, looking to her phone to check the time and deciding against sitting. "It's just that it doesn't go with a chocolate donut."

"I like what I like," Gabe said with a shrug. Then he tapped on his phone and said, "I texted you."

"I saw that," Hayden said, as if it was interesting, but not something to be discussed at any length. "Ready to go in?"

"No but yes," Gabe answered. His eyes flickered to the entrance of the Crafters Guild, the unassuming stone building where the Wardens went about their business. It looked like a cross between a brownstone apartment building and a bank. It had a large front door with brass fittings, and imposing glass windows tinted black. Gabe gulped the last of his orange juice and savored the last bite of his donut, then cleaned his table and started to walk toward the Crafters Guild.

"Wait," Hayden said.

"Why?" he asked, but the answer became obvious when she stepped forward and hugged him. Her hair whispered across his cheek. The hug was brief, but solid, and then she stepped away.

"I'm nervous," she explained. "Needed that." Before Gabe could reply, she was on her way to the door, and he was still dazedly standing with the pigeons when she had the door open and was gesturing for him to hurry.

Inside, they walked across a tile floor, their feet tap-tapping with their steps, and showed their identification cards to a receptionist at the front desk.

"Gabe Basuldua and Hayden Fracasso?" she said, looking

to her computer. "Ah, yes. You're both Trainers, right?" The woman was in her late twenties, a redhead with bobbed hair and sizeable glasses, dressed like she was ready for a picnic, while the two security guards standing behind her looked like they were ready for war. Bulletproof vests. Full helmets with visors. Leather gloves. No visible skin. Gabe nodded to them, but there wasn't any reply.

"We're Trainers," Hayden said. "Correct." Trainers were the people in charge of preparing monsters for battle. Hayden was proud to be one.

"You can go up," the receptionist said. "They're expecting you on the second floor." She touched a button on her desk, and a pair of elevator doors opened.

Hayden called out, "Thanks," as she and Gabe got in the elevator. A series of sensors swept over them, scanning for anything of suspicious nature. Hayden wondered what would happen if something was found. Would the elevator plummet to some underground prison? She tried to look innocent, but was as nervous as when they'd raised the vampire from his coffin, or during the private overnight flight from Wales to Seattle. The vampire had claimed the window seat and watched the clouds and the ocean below, fascinated at how technology had progressed during the centuries he'd slumbered, and equally fascinated by the throats of the two flight attendants, eyeing them hungrily despite having already dined on several blood bags. The blood, Hayden knew, had come from volunteers and been supplied by the Crafters Guild. Count Drustan had complained it was stale.

As the sensors faded and the elevator began rising, Hayden thought of the cabin on the lake, and explaining the security systems to Count Drustan, how he was forbidden to leave and all the various precautions that prevented him from even attempting it. Hayden remembered her shock when the vampire had raised the curtains and let the sun shine through the cabin's windows. Count Drustan had told her to close her surprised, open mouth and explained that—thanks to his unthinkable age—sunlight was little more than an irritant to him. Gabe had then taught Count Drustan all about the television and video games. The vampire had been enthralled and promised to behave. Five hours after they'd left the vampire to travel to Tacoma for this meeting, a guard at the cabin called to report how, despite tripping none of the alarms and setting off none of the security precautions, Count Drustan had slipped out of the cabin and was feasting on a freshly killed bear, which he'd snuck into the living room by some impossible means, drinking the bear's blood while playing *Dragon Quest*.

"The trouble with vampires," Hayden told Gabe as the elevator made a slow journey to the second floor, "is that they're not only incredibly powerful; they can be vastly intelligent as well."

Gabe didn't say anything.

"Sorry," Hayden said. "I had some things churning around in my head, and I needed to get them out." Gabe nodded at that, just as the elevator opened on the second floor. They were met by a pair of security guards who motioned them to a door. Gabe walked to the door, grabbed the handle, and then looked to Hayden. She nodded at him.

He took a deep breath and opened the door.

CHAPTER 6

Inside, they found an office boardroom, with two women and a man seated on the opposite side of a long oval table. They each had open laptops, along with glasses of water from a large pitcher beaded with condensation. The walls displayed framed maps of the world. The older of the two women gestured for Hayden and Gabe to be seated.

"Welcome," she told them as they took their chairs. She was a white woman in her sixties, but still looked like she could take on a monster, if necessary, and was wearing a stylish red suit. "My name is Meeda Obermark. I understand you're here to register for a Versus battle and that you have a vampire?"

"We do," Hayden answered eagerly. "Count Drustan. He's at a cabin near Lake Chelan. We'd like to register as quickly as possible. I'm not sure we can hold him there for long."

"My dear," Meeda said with a smile, "you can't hold a vampire at all. Not one of Drustan's power, anywise. Not unless he's game for the battle. Did you tell him about the werewolf?"

"We did," Gabe said.

"Then all will be well, I'd think. Vampires love to fight werewolves. He wouldn't dare miss the chance. Still, no reason to delay registering. I have your files in front of me"—she tapped her laptop computer—"so let me verify your information. Interrupt me if I'm wrong."

She waited for Gabe and Hayden to nod. They did, with Gabe looking to the other adults at the table. One was a white woman in her early forties, at Gabe's best guess, and he also guessed she was Meeda's daughter. The resemblance was just too similar. She was dressed in a black suit with a large bumblebee brooch on her chest. The other adult was a bearded Black man in his late twenties, wearing a frayed turtleneck sweater and glasses with bright green frames.

"Oh," Meeda said, noticing Gabe's interest in the others. "Yes. I should do introductions. This is Carter Addo"—she gestured to the man—"an expert on communications and folklore. And next to him is my daughter, Quinn Obermark, who—I dare say—is the world's foremost expert on mummies. Sometimes I think she'd marry one, if given the chance."

"Mother," Quinn said in a scolding tone.

"Yes," Meeda said, holding back a smile. "We must behave in front of the children." She took a drink and then told Hayden and Gabe, "I'm sure you know these next bits, but it's policy to spit them out into the open. I am a Crafter. Mid-rank. I know a few magics. Semi-impressive ways to bend reality. I'm useful at parties but not as much in the field. Management is my strong point. Quinn and Carter are both Wardens. Dependable. Highly trained. But no magics, or at least only the murmurs of magics."

"No bending of reality from me." Quinn shrugged. "Can't even make it quiver."

"Splendid Wardens, the both of them," Meeda said. "Together, we Crafters and Wardens manage a vast, but secret, global network of people who bring together a wide range of monsters so that these creatures may battle one another. Trainers, such as yourselves, are kept, um, *mostly* safe from these monsters thanks to incredibly rare medallions. It's your job to lead these monsters, letting them prove themselves against one another, because monsters *want* to fight. It's in their nature. It's how they socialize. Monsters were the primary founders of our organization, and we honor them with our efforts. You already know everything I've told you, correct?"

"Correct," Gabe said.

"Yes," Hayden agreed. "But, I mean, only about the Versus battles. I didn't know you were a Crafter. I thought you were only a Warden."

"Being a Warden is not an 'only' situation," Meeda said, with the slightest of frowns. "Wardens are just as important as Crafters. If you remove *any* parts from an engine, then the engine doesn't run."

"Oh," Hayden said, embarrassed, looking to Quinn and Carter. "Of course. Sorry."

"Not a problem," Carter said, but in a voice that said there might have been a trace of hurt feelings. Hayden was glad when Meeda changed the subject.

"Now then, let's commence," Meeda said, tapping her nails on her laptop. "The two of you are registering a vampire, Count Drustan, to fight a werewolf acquired by . . . Tradd Risso and Joon Baker. Do you know them?" She looked up from her laptop.

"A little," Hayden answered.

"We actually met them here," Gabe said. "Researching in your library. Maybe a year ago. We talked a little. They seemed . . . nice enough, I guess? It'll be too bad to kick their butts. Or, kick their werewolf's butt, I guess."

"Confident of a win?" Meeda asked.

"Yes," Hayden said. She thought about qualifying her answer, but . . . a yes would suffice.

"Good," Meeda said. "A positive attitude is half the battle. Although it must be said that fangs and claws are the other half. Let's move on to you two, personally." Her eyes flickered down to her laptop as she read out, "Hayden Fall Fracasso. Nine years old. Your father is a game designer who . . . worked on *World of Warcraft*? Impressive. And your mother is a comic book artist? You have a very creative family."

"My parents are weird," Hayden said, then felt her cheeks reddening and hurriedly added, "I meant that in a good way."

"No need to worry," Meeda said. "That's the way I took it." She glanced to her computer and frowned, adding, "Oh, I see your parents are divorced. I hadn't noticed that at first. I'm sorry."

"They're still friends," Hayden said. This wasn't a topic she enjoyed talking about. "They only live a few miles apart. I have rooms at both houses. They still love each other but not, you know, the way they did. They both still love me, though." She wasn't sure why she'd added that last part and wished she hadn't.

"I'm sure they do," Meeda said. "Let's continue with you, Gabe." She looked to him, and he nodded, not sure if he was supposed to speak.

Meeda said, "Gabe Sylvester Basuldua. Age nine. Your dad is a baseball coach for Linfield University. Your mother, Sandra, is an estate librarian who catalogs rare books. Interesting. I'd love to discuss some of her finds."

"She *loves* talking about books," Gabe said. "Our house is full of them. We have a first edition of *Dracula*."

"On that note," Meeda said. "Let's talk about vampires, shall we? Are the two of you certain you can control Count Drustan?"

"Yes," Gabe said.

"No," Hayden said. The two of them stopped and looked at each other.

"A difference of opinion," Quinn noted. "Interesting."

Hayden said, "Well, what you said earlier got me to thinking. You said we can only control Count Drustan as long as it serves his purposes. When we dug him out of his crypt, he was—oh, crackers—*so* scary! I felt like a mouse in front of a cat. But when we told him about fighting the werewolf, he changed. He's felt, uh, friendly ever since."

"A friendly vampire," Quinn said, in a tone of disbelief.

"I'm not forgetting what he is," Hayden argued. "That's why I said I'm not sure we can control him. I'm not forgetting the power he had when he first floated out of his coffin, and I'm not forgetting how—at the time—he was at his *weakest* for hundreds of years. Now that he's had blood, he's even more powerful. So, no, we can't control him. But we *can* lead him to fight the werewolf, because, if this makes sense, we're only leading him to where he already wants to go."

"I'm changing my answer," Gabe said. "I agree with Hayden."

"I think we all do," Carter said. "And I, for one, think we can go ahead and sign the registration papers. You have a vampire, and the right attitude, and you're fully qualified."

"Agreed," Quinn said. Everyone turned to look at Meeda for her opinion, understanding that her single vote was worth more than everyone else's together. But at that moment, there was a faint scream from below, and the whole building shivered. Red lights flashed. Alarms rang out. The walls shivered again. It felt like a series of explosions were going off below. The floor shook and bulged upward.

"Red alert," a man's voice announced through the intercom, straining to remain calm. "Red alert. Subject One is loose on the first floor. Repeat, *Subject One is loose*."

"Oh, you're *kidding* me!" Carter spat out. His eyes were wide.

"I *told* them!" Quinn hissed. Her brow was furrowed.

"Subject One?" Hayden asked. She heard gunshots from somewhere, and intense electrical cracklings, like a giant hornet's buzz.

"You're not cleared to know!" Carter told Hayden, hurrying out the door.

"It's Ptahhotep," Quinn said, standing, rummaging through her pockets, and then bringing out a trio of carved turquoise scarab beetles. "These were his. Found tucked away inside his bandages when he was discovered." Another seeming explosion rocked the building. Quinn fought for balance, and one of the scarabs fell to the floor. Gabe picked it up and handed it back to her.

"You . . . *discovered* Ptahhotep?" he asked Quinn, who took a deep breath and looked to her mother, obviously asking for permission to explain. Meeda nodded. Quinn looked back to Gabe and said, "Ptahhotep was a vizier during the reign of Djedkare Isesi, an Egyptian Pharaoh from the Old Kingdom, well over four thousand years ago."

"You mean . . . ?" Hayden said.

"Yes," Quinn said, hurrying out the door. "Ptahhotep is a mummy. And he's on the loose."

CHAPTER 7

"Stay here," Meeda ordered Hayden and Gabe, who were getting up to follow the group.

"But, we can *help*!" Hayden argued.

"Thanks, but we're well equipped to deal with an escaped mummy."

"If that were true," Gabe said, "then Ptahhotep wouldn't have escaped in the first place." This earned him a frown from Meeda, but it was brief, and then she admitted, "Not altogether wrong." Another shiver trembled through the building, and a framed map of Australia fell off the wall, the glass shattering. And then came a flurry of those strange, intense, electrical hums.

"What's that noise?" Gabe asked.

"Shock prods. Powerful enough to bring Ptahhotep down. It's worked before."

"He's escaped *before*?" Hayden asked, as the floor shook yet again.

"Twice," Meeda acknowledged. Another seeming explosion rocked the building as she spoke.

"He's obviously dangerous," Hayden said. "Why do you keep him here?" She was trying to remain calm amid all the booming concussions, the sharp electrical bursts, the frantic screams from the floor below, and one long moan of rage that was clearly the mummy.

"The Egyptian division of the Crafters Guild is currently being rebuilt," Meeda said, "so when Ptahhotep was discovered, they asked if we could keep him for a time." She paused as the walls and floor rumbled again, shaking with the sheer power of the mummy rampaging below, on the building's first floor. "We tried to house him at Pensworth, but his presence made the other mummies riot."

"Riot?" Hayden asked.

"Pensworth?" Gabe questioned.

"Riot, yes. There are six other mummies at Pensworth, and they all teamed up in an escape attempt. We've never seen mummies work together before. It was . . . odd. And, to answer your question, Gabe, Pensworth is a holding facility."

"Is that a nice way of saying it's a prison?"

"No. If it was a prison, I'd have said it was a prison. Pensworth is more like a school to help monsters understand modern culture and society, both their own and that of humanity." As she spoke, the screams from the floor below became more audible, even as the alarm claxons roared and the lights flashed red.

"We have a breach," the man on the intercom called out, no longer masking his panic. "We have a breach! *A breach!*"

"Breach?" Hayden asked.

"It's . . . he's almost made it outside," Meeda said, adding a burst of cursing as red as the lights. She looked to the door, and then to Hayden and Gabe, and said, "Listen. I have to go. And *you* have to promise you'll stay here. Can you do that?"

"Well . . . ," Gabe began, but then the floor and walls rumbled again, and the center of the floor collapsed. Gabe threw himself and Hayden against the wall to avoid the now gaping hole, but Meeda wasn't as lucky and was sent tumbling down below in an avalanche of concrete and wood. Staring in shock through the hole, Hayden had a quick glimpse of Meeda sprawled atop the fallen debris— and of a tattered, smoldering mummy, badly singed by all the electrical attacks, hurling guards aside. A collapsing chunk of concrete the size of a small fridge smashed onto his shoulders. He barely staggered, grunting with a sound that Gabe felt like a physical force, and then the mummy looked up. They locked eyes for a moment before the mummy disappeared from view as the cloud of dust from the collapsed floor billowed upward like a tangible fog.

"We have to help," Gabe said, looking to Hayden.

"Of course we do," she said, already crawling down the edges of the huge hole in the floor, holding on to a broken pipe that was spewing water, feeling it bend with her weight, which was nice because it served to lower her even more. Gabe scrambled to join her, pushing the huge wooden table—balanced precariously at the edge of the hole—the rest of the way into the void so that one end thumped to a stop on the debris pile below. This acted as a steep ramp that Gabe slid down, whooshing into the billowing smoke and dust, which was alive with flashes of light and screams from unseen soldiers. Gabe skidded to a stop on some concrete shards, finding his balance just in time for Hayden's feet to swing only inches past his face, her legs kicking about as she tried to lower herself from above. Gabe grabbed her legs, wanting to help.

"Is that you or a mummy?" Hayden shrieked. It was nearly impossible to see, what with everything that was happening, the nearly solid dust cloud, and the flashes of blue light from the electrical prods. "I said . . . is that Gabe or Ptahhotep? *Please* don't be a four-thousand-year-old engine of destruction!"

"I'm only nine!" Gabe called up, steadying Hayden's legs. "Mom *does* think I'm an engine of destruction, though!" Hayden's feet slid past him, and she appeared fully from the smoke, hurtling down, but he was ready for her and helped to slow her fall.

"Do you see Meeda?" Hayden asked, balanced on the rubble.

"There she is!" Gabe said, pointing. The dust was beginning to settle, and the smoke was clearing. Meeda was still sprawled atop a slab of broken concrete, obviously dazed, with blood on the side of her head. Gabe began hurrying as best as possible over the uneven rubble to help the fallen woman, but then, from the dust . . .

The mummy.

CHAPTER 8

The mummy was only five and a half feet tall, but still seemed enormous. Gabe could feel the power radiating out from beneath the yellowed bandages, which were spotted with charred marks and showed glimpses of decayed flesh, dark tans and ruddy blacks. The mummy's presence felt like being struck by a tidal wave, and the surrounding air reminded Gabe of whenever he opened the freezer at home, releasing that cold rush of air.

The mummy stepped closer.

"Peanuts," Gabe cursed, stepping back, his gaze locked on the red eyes of a man who'd died thousands of years in the past. The mummy stepped forward, moving beneath the spill from the water pipe, closer to Gabe, who was making sure he didn't make any sudden moves or threatening gestures. Wary of even turning his head, he saw from the edges of his eyes that Hayden was helping Meeda to her feet.

"Gabe," Hayden said. "Get away from the mummy."

"Yeah," he agreed. "That'd be nice." But if he moved, he might draw the mummy's attention and cause him to attack, and that would be Bad. The monster stepped out from beneath the torrent of water from the broken pipe. Thoroughly soaked, the mummy's bandages stuck even closer to his flesh. Small bits of ice formed on him, dangling like tiny icicles from his dressings.

Hayden slipped. She'd been trying to guide the dazed Meeda off the piled rubble from the collapsed floor, but a chunk of concrete twisted beneath her feet and she nearly went down, gasping in shock. Ptahhotep's attention snapped in her direction. The mummy let loose a roar of rage that billowed the loose tatters of his bandages. His red eyes flared brighter. Kicking concrete aside, he began striding for Meeda. And Hayden.

He only took three steps before a baseball-size chunk of concrete thumped off the back of his head. The impact was hard enough to stun a regular man, and would probably knock him unconscious or worse, but the mummy barely seemed to notice. His stride didn't alter. It wasn't until the second chunk of concrete hit him that he thought to look back, and in looking back he took the third chunk of concrete in his face.

"Grahh," Ptahhotep moaned in irritation, staring at Gabe. Then the mummy's gaze swept to Hayden and Meeda, and then back again to Gabe, who settled the mummy's decision by hurling another chunk of concrete, this one bouncing off the mummy's chest. Red eyes flaring, he turned away from Hayden . . .

"Yes!" Gabe said. "It worked!"

. . . and began walking toward Gabe.

"Oh, dang," Gabe muttered. "That worked." A chunk of concrete puffed into dust beneath the mummy's foot, crushed not by the mummy's weight, but by his sheer ancient power.

Gabe was in trouble.

He looked around the room. There were three doors, although one of them—the door to the main lobby—was fully blocked by the collapsed rubble. Another was strewn with unconscious guards, a few with broken arms or legs. Carter—the man they'd met on the second floor—was among the fallen, barely stirring, one hand holding his head. The red lights and the churning roar of the alarms served to deaden Gabe's thoughts. He reached down for one of the fallen shock prods, a baton the length of a baseball bat, but couldn't understand how to get it to work. It was little more than a stick against an ancient creature whose willpower had defied death itself.

The mummy stepped closer.

Sweat trickled into Gabe's eyes, stinging them with salt.

The creature's hands rose, reaching out for Gabe, exposing tattered fingers, withered and discolored.

Gabe raised his baton, ready to defend himself, but at that

point two more guards rushed into the room, including a woman with a modified shotgun that fired an electrified net out over the mummy, clinging to him with hundreds of tiny hooks. A powerful surge of electricity flashed along a cord to the net, sparks flying. The mummy fell, rolling on the floor in agony, crushing concrete shards and splashing through the puddles from the burst pipes. But then, almost too quick to see, the mummy grasped the net and pulled. The shotgun was ripped from the woman's hands, and, attached to the cord, snapped through the air like a whip, striking her partner, who fell heavily. The trapped mummy burst from the net, its hooks stripping away fragments of his bandages, revealing more of the ancient dried flesh.

Free of the net, Ptahhotep stomped on the floor, shattering the concrete and sending out a wave of concussive force that hurled the woman and her injured partner against the wall, spinning them across the floor like leaves on a street. Gabe lost his balance and fell, feeling like he'd been struck by a hundred invisible fists. The boardroom table slid farther into the hole and crashed to one side, with Hayden and Meeda, hobbling out of its path, sent sprawling by the impact. Dust billowed up from all around, with pulverized concrete reduced to nothing but a cloud in the air, choking Gabe's throat and lungs. On all fours, he couldn't stop coughing, and the dust was burning in his eyes. By the time he was able to recover, the mummy was standing over him.

"Ah, peanuts," Gabe said.

He tried to appear like he wasn't a threat, which wasn't a challenge, since he was still on all fours, and even the simple act of breathing triggered violent bouts of coughing.

The mummy reached for him, but Gabe rolled out of the way, scrambling to his feet. The mummy was lumbering, but like a locomotive once he'd built up steam. Again and again, Gabe desperately tried to avoid contact, staggering even when the mummy missed, because Ptahhotep's mere presence shook the very walls. The mummy was enraged. And tireless. Gabe was covered in dust and sweat, knowing he couldn't last much longer. Soon, he'd be too exhausted to move.

The mummy reached for him again. Gabe couldn't catch his breath. Couldn't dodge. This was it. He felt the tattered bandages of Ptahhotep's fingers touch his cheek, the withered flesh so close that Gabe could smell it. It was a ripe, charnel smell. A dusty slaughterhouse. Gabe couldn't will his exhausted legs to budge. He closed his eyes.

"Stop!" he heard, and opened his eyes to see Quinn, Meeda's daughter, hurrying into the room, holding out the three scarab beetles from before.

"I command you!" she yelled. "You must do as I say, ancient one!" In reply, the roaring mummy picked up a chunk of concrete as large as Gabe and hurled it at Quinn. Gasping in horror, she ducked low. The concrete soared over her head and smashed into a wall. One of the scarabs fell from her grasp, and she shouted in dismay as it toppled into a crevice between shards of rubble.

"Oh crap!" she said. "Gabe! Help me! These scarabs are the only things that can control Ptahhotep!"

"*This* is being controlled?" Gabe asked in disbelief. The mummy stomped toward Quinn, bellowing in rage and fury, shaking the walls. Gabe spotted the fallen scarab and snaked his hand down between the rubble, his fingers barely touching the cold surface of the ancient artifact. He could hear Quinn shouting in some language he didn't understand, and Hayden was doing the same. Ancient Egyptian, Gabe realized. The two of them were trying to reach the mummy by speaking in a language it could recognize. The only thing Gabe recognized, though, was that if he didn't get to that scarab beetle before the mummy got to Quinn, they were all doomed. The mummy was now speaking in ancient Egyptian as well, his words cold, dusty, and unthinkably angry.

The mummy was only a few feet from Quinn. From Hayden.

Finally, Gabe's fingers closed on the scarab. "Yes!" he yelled in triumph, hurriedly handing it to Quinn. She nodded a frantic thanks and held out all three scarabs, yelling for Ptahhotep to stop, ordering him by the power of the scarabs.

But Gabe could see in the mummy's red eyes that it wasn't working. He could see that the mummy couldn't be stopped. He could see that they were all doomed.

A hand reached out and snagged the scarabs from an astonished Quinn's grasp. But it wasn't Ptahhotep's hand. It was Hayden's.

"Oh, my gosh and crackers," she said in a tone of disgust, holding the scarabs, looking not to the mummy but to Quinn. "Don't you understand what he's saying?"

"Uh, a little?" Quinn said.

"*Seriously*," Hayden said, turning away from Quinn. "Your ancient Egyptian is terrible. You need more practice." With that, Hayden walked forward and faced the mummy. Ptahhotep was barely taller than her, but still seemed to be a giant. His lips, equally as crusty as his bandages, snarled and twisted in rage.

"Here," Hayden said, and she held out her fist and said something Gabe couldn't understand, speaking in ancient Egyptian even as she opened her hand to reveal the three scarabs.

The mummy's expression changed. His eyes, so recently full of rage, calmed. One hand went limp to his side even as a huge sigh escaped his lungs, a billowing of dried air blowing at the bandages around his mouth. He took the scarabs from Hayden, his touch gentle, his eyes moving back and forth between the scarabs and Hayden, who smiled and nodded at him.

For a few moments, Ptahhotep studied the scarabs in his hand. Then he tucked them inside the bandages of his chest, sat on the floor, slid to one side, and began to sleep.

The room certainly didn't grow quiet. There were still the concrete groans of the ruined ceiling above. Still the moans of the injured. The shrieking alarms. But compared to the recent roar of the mummy—now reduced to nothing but soft breaths—it felt almost silent. That meant it was easy for everyone to hear, this time, when Hayden spoke.

"Seriously," she said again, frowning at Quinn. "Poor Ptahhotep was dead for thousands of years, and the first thing you do when he rises from his tomb is steal his scarabs? I'd be mad, too."

CHAPTER 9

"I'm so excited I get to fight a *vampire!*" the werewolf said with a grin. He wasn't currently in werewolf form, though. His name was Redd Sampayo, and he presently appeared entirely human, a Latino man in his midthirties wearing blue jeans and a black shirt. No shoes. No socks. He had a thick beard and full sideburns but wasn't markedly hairier than average. Despite that, he still gave off the feeling of a predatory beast. Every move he made felt like a threat.

"Yes," Joon said. "Werewolf versus vampire. Kind of a classic battle, honestly." She and Redd, along with Tradd, were in Joemma Beach State Park, walking along the salty waters of the Puget Sound not far from Tacoma. The beach was less sandy than pebble-y, and Joon was enjoying the crunch of the stones beneath her shoes, the lapping of the small waves, and an occasional crab scurrying away from their approach.

"I'm still having trouble believing it," Redd said, "that you took me from my personal forest in order to participate in a Versus battle against a deadly bloodsucking monster."

"Well," Tradd said, "when you put it that way, it sounds kind of weird."

"But correct," Joon added.

"Yeah," Tradd said. "Correct."

"Well, I'm all for it," Redd said, dipping his toes in the cold water. "This sounds like an absolute gas."

"Good," Tradd said. "I bet you feel bad about hunting us in your forest, now."

"Oh, not at all. That was absolutely hilarious. I still laugh thinking about your faces. Joon, hold my shirt, would you?"

"What?" Joon asked, but Redd was already taking off his shirt, handing it to her. The fabric was warm. Like it had just come out of a dryer. "What am I supposed to do with this?"

"I'm going swimming."

"The water's cold," Tradd said. "It's almost always cold here."

"So what? I'm warm-blooded." He waded shin-deep into the water and turned back. "What's the purpose of this fight, anyway? Me versus a vampire? I mean, from your side of things. On the drive here, you were saying something about Crafters? Wardens? Who are these people? Calling them Wardens makes it sound like you're going to be putting me in jail." He paused, and fur began sprouting all along his arms and over his chest. His eyes narrowed. "You're not tricking me, are you? You're not gonna have me fight just to put me in jail afterward?"

"Just the opposite, actually," Joon said, still holding the shirt and still not knowing what to do with it. She handed it to Tradd. He gave her a frown. "You'll have more freedom than ever. More friends. The Versus battles take place all over the world, with, oh, gosh, just all sorts of creatures."

"Okay," Redd said. "Go on." He stood tall and sniffed the air.

Tradd said, "Greater society forces creatures like you, along with vampires and all the others, into hiding. And that's terrible for your mental health. So the Crafters and the Wardens work together to safely incorporate you into, um, maybe not society as a whole, but *a* society, at least."

"Having me fight a vampire is your idea of *safely incorporating* me into a society?" He waded farther out into the water.

"It is," Joon said. "A little, anyway. Would you have responded if we'd emailed you an invite to a tea party?"

"Maybe. If there was a good fight involved—so I guess that proves your point. Okay, so you're getting me out of my house. My forest. My warehouse. Whatever. Very nice of you. But who are the Crafters? The Wardens?"

"The Crafters are the ones who make these," Joon said, holding up her werewolf medallion to show Redd.

"How are they made?" Redd asked. His fur was still sprouting, but the changes were slow. He was still a man, mostly. Just slightly taller. Slightly more muscular. Very much hairier.

"We don't really know," Tradd said. He found a stick and speared it down into the pebble-strewn beach. Once he was certain it was secure, he hung Redd's shirt from it. "The process is a secret. The leader of the Crafters is always a witch, and she passes the technique down to her successor, time after time."

"So those things are magic, huh?" Redd asked. He was watching his fingers growing, lengthening. An extra joint appeared. Fingernails turned to claws.

"Yes," Joon said. "Probably. Or at least made *with* magic. The secrets are pretty well kept." She sat on the beach and stretched out her legs. The whole day felt surreal. A werewolf in the waves.

"And the Wardens?" Redd asked.

"They work with the Crafters. There's a lot more Wardens than Crafters. A support team. The Board of Wardens has a werewolf, actually."

"A werewolf?" Redd asked. His voice was getting deeper.

"And a gnome. A type of fairy. I hear they're trying to get more creatures on the board. Representation of culture is important."

"That's what everyone is trying to do," Tradd said. "Keep the culture of monsters alive. When Joon and I had to hunt for the medallions, and research where you might be found, we were learning all about you and other werewolves. Learning about your culture."

"Good for you," Redd said. His jawline was elongating. His words were mocking.

He added, "Although it *would* be nice, I guess, to learn more about my world. The world beneath *your* world." His words were more thoughtful, now. His head was flattening, lengthening. Looking more like a werewolf than a man, Redd strode farther out into the water. Up to his waist, now.

Joon said, "Your world is *barely* beneath our world. And honestly, sometimes it's not at all. Sometimes monsters are in plain sight. Such incidents are part of what we call the Great Bubble-Up, the times when human society merges with the less defined society of monsters."

"Vampires are always bubbling up into humanity," Tradd said. "I suppose they *need* to, if they're going to drink blood."

"Every human culture has discovered monsters in their midst," Joon said. "Fairies in England. A whole range of creatures in Japan. You're not the first monster I've met. I met some, um, goblins, once. It didn't go well. And I met a woman, sort of, named Killian."

"Sort of?" Redd asked.

"She's a dryad. A nymph. A tree spirit. Some would even say she's a minor goddess. I found a dryad medallion, and then I found her. She's eventually going to fight a witch. But that's in the future. We're still trying to find a proper matchup. But never mind all that for now. We were talking about the Versus battles and how they give monsters something to do without, uh . . ." Her words trailed off.

"Wreaking havoc on humanity?" Redd said.

"Yeah. Sorry."

"Nobody likes havoc," Redd acknowledged, but then added, "I do like *causing* a bit of havoc, though." He was fully a werewolf, now. Tradd watched the transformation with fascination. He knew others were watching, too. There were hidden Wardens in the forest, just past the beach, keeping a close eye on the werewolf in case anything went wrong.

"So, what do you two get out of this?" the werewolf asked. "Money?"

"We get the medallions," Tradd said, holding his up. The sun glinted from his red, round glasses.

"You already *have* the medallions," the werewolf noted. He was up to his chest, now, arms waving through the water at his sides.

"We get to *keep* the medallions," Joon clarified. "Whenever we Trainers find a medallion, we can lead a monster—whichever one is depicted on the medallion—into battle, and if our monster wins, we can keep the medallion. If not, the Wardens take it away."

"What do these thieving Wardens do with your stolen medallions?" Redd asked. He was swimming, now, back and forth, with long strokes of his long arms. Joon was surprised. She'd never thought of werewolves in the water before, but she supposed that since wolves can swim, and men can swim, why not a wolfman?

Tradd said, "Give them to the teams in battles, but, uh, the other teams."

"I thought if you were in a Versus battle, you already had medallions?" Redd had caught a fish and was gnawing on it, raw, ripping off shreds and gulping them down.

"Tradd means the Trainers on the *other* side," Joon said, trying not to watch the fish carnage. "Tradd and I already have werewolf medallions, but when you fight Count Drustan—that's his name—we'll be issued vampire medallions as well. Only for the duration of the battle, though. And since we don't have any real bond with the vampire, our medallions won't be as powerful, but they *should* be enough to protect us from Count Drustan, if he goes berserk."

"Vampires always go berserk," the werewolf said between gulps of herring. "So, are these other kids going to have werewolf medallions, then?"

"Yes," Tradd said.

"And you call yourselves Trainers? You and Joon?"

"That's what we're called. Yes. Crafters. Wardens. And Trainers."

"Seems like this is all a big game to you people," the werewolf snarled. It was difficult to tell if he was angry, though. Everything he said was a snarl.

"It's not a game," Joon said. "At all. There are entire monster cultures at risk. Yes, some creatures live in groups, but overall monsters are quite isolated. We're doing our best to keep the society of monsters alive. Everyone in the human world wants to sweep werewolves and vampires and mermaids and all the others into the trash cans of history. What we want—"

"I don't care what you want," Redd said. "I only care about fighting. I can't wait to fight a vampire. Never fought one. I'm excited." Treading water, he leaned back and howled. Joon watched the water rippling around him from the sonic boom of his call.

The werewolf plunged underwater. Seconds ticked away. A minute. Then two. Tradd and Joon looked at each other, wondering, scanning the water, looking for air bubbles. Joon clutched the medallion in her hand, wanting to keep it, wanting it to be hers, knowing that she would lose it if the vampire beat her werewolf, but what would happen to her medallion if the werewolf simply . . . drowned?

Three minutes passed by. Four. Tradd rubbed nervously at his medallion. He didn't want to lose his werewolf. He needed to win the fight. There was too much at stake. They hadn't told Redd the whole truth. For the Trainers, there were prizes involved if they earned enough medallions. Life-changing rewards. Tradd found that he was holding his own breath, waiting for the werewolf to surface from the waters of the Puget Sound.

"It's been . . . a long time," Joon said, voicing her fear. Five minutes had passed. Six. Joon considered the Wardens hidden in the forest, waiting and watching. Should she call them for help? Should she jump into the water and search for the werewolf? What should she do? More time passed. Seven minutes. Eight.

When her phone rang, Joon almost screamed. She dropped her werewolf medallion and then frantically grabbed it up while looking to her phone. It was the Wardens calling. They'd been watching, of course. Was she in trouble for losing her werewolf, for maybe . . . letting him drown?

"Hello?" she answered while looking with worried eyes to Tradd. He bit his lip, breathing slow, watching her.

"Joon," a voice came from the phone. It was deep and gravelly. Raw and primal. The werewolf's voice.

"Werewolf?" Joon said in a questioning voice. "Redd?"

Tradd, still watching her, grew confused, silently mouthing her own words. *Werewolf? Redd?*

"Yeah, it's me," came the voice from the phone. "I thought it might be funny to sneak out of the water and stalk the two Wardens I kept smelling, but this one peed himself, and they both passed out. Could you come and wake them up or something?"

"Ooookay," Joon said, drawing out the word because she didn't know how else to respond.

"And bring me another herring," the werewolf snarled. "I'm hungry."

CHAPTER 10

The monsters were gone. Redd was staying in a cabin on one side of Lake Chelan, and Count Drustan was on the opposite shore. Tradd knew the two monsters would soon be given a preview of the Tacoma location where their battle would take place, but today it was time for him and Joon to prepare. They'd be training along with Gabe Basuldua and Hayden Fracasso, the other team, who could—in the near future—be responsible for him losing his werewolf medallion.

Tradd sat across from Joon in the empty Meadowcamp Grade School cafeteria. Stashing his phone in his pocket—having just been telling his dad about the school where he was at and the training that was to come—he took off his glasses and rubbed his eyes, then put them back on and looked around the cafeteria, with its posters showcasing the importance of nutrition and hygiene and being kind to others.

"What about the importance of keeping your medallions?" Tradd muttered, speaking in a barely audible voice because he and Joon weren't alone in the cafeteria. Gabe and Hayden were sitting on the other side, keeping to themselves, isolated, like monsters on opposite sides of a lake.

Tradd was trying his best to ignore the presence of the other team, absently rolling his medallion over the table while eating scrambled eggs and a waffle with thick syrup. He could hear the Wardens at work in the school's adjoining gymnasium as they prepared it for this morning's practice. There were no other people in the school. It was the weekend. The students were gone. Tradd was, to be honest, a little sad that nobody else was there. It would've been nice to make some new friends. It would be nice, also, to keep his werewolf medallion. He traced a finger over the edge of it, frowning.

"They'll really take our medallions if we lose?" he asked Joon.

"We won't lose," she said, which wasn't really an answer, but was totally an answer. Tradd nodded, still rolling his medallion over the table. It clinked into his plate. Toppled over. He picked up his medallion—*his* medallion—and clicked it back onto its chain. He needed this medallion. He needed *more* medallions. Two more, to be precise.

Three medallions and he could make a request from the Crafters. That was what they'd left out while talking to

Redd the day before. Three medallions—three medallions that were his and that couldn't be taken away—and he could, in effect, make a wish. One that would be granted if it was within the power of the Crafters. Or the monsters depicted on those three medallions.

Tradd's intended wish was simple. Three years ago, his dog, Keeper, had gone missing. A kitchen door left open. The terrier had always been inquisitive, always seeking new adventures. Tradd had watched the video from his porch's surveillance camera a hundred times. Keeper stepping outside. Keeper roaming the yard. Keeper gone. The dog had only been two years old. He could still be alive. Tradd wanted to find him.

What Joon wanted was to be a witch. She wanted to learn how to bend the laws of reality. Magic at her fingertips. Tradd wanted that for her. He did. But mostly he wanted his dog back.

He studied the silver werewolf medallion. It represented one-third of the way to the finish line, but *only* if he could keep it.

That meant his werewolf needed to win.

"Ready?" Quinn Obermark asked Hayden, who looked up from the table to the Warden. Quinn was dressed in black slacks with a yellow blouse, with a bumblebee-shaped pin in her hair. She wobbled her phone back and forth and said, "I'm told the gym is prepared."

"Pretty sure we're ready?" Hayden answered, looking to Gabe, who nodded. They were ready.

Hayden stood from her half-eaten breakfast and felt the gold medallion in her pocket. She'd wanted a vampire medallion for a long time, and wanted to *keep* this one. She thought of the Medallion Wish Board she'd made in shop class at school, shaping the walnut wood into a circle as big as a hula hoop, adding hooks from where medallions could be hung, labeling them with the names of the medallions she wanted to find. A ghost medallion. A minotaur medallion. A zombie medallion and many more, including a unicorn medallion, although good luck with *that*. Mostly, though, she was incredibly pleased to have found the vampire medallions. Who wouldn't want a vampire? Okay, Count Drustan did rather terrify her, but the fear was worth it if it meant she won the Versus battle and could truly *keep* her medallion.

Hayden had another pair of medallions, too, but wasn't sure what they were. A griffin, maybe? The medallions she'd found were so old that they were terribly worn, the figures indistinct. She'd spent countless hours researching what they might be, and was willing to spend countless more. Having two medallions and winning two Versus battles was a lot more than simply winning one. If she could keep *one* medallion, she'd be started on the path. If she won *two*, she was almost to the finish line.

There was a commotion near the front door. Six Wardens escorting a large rolling cage. A strange squawking sound. Gabe saw a flash of something leathery in the cage, which was the size of a van. A musky scent filled the cafeteria. Something in the cage stood up. Hissed. A beak came slashing out, but the Wardens escorting the cage were well back. Gabe gasped at what he saw.

"Was that . . . ?" he asked, unable to even form the word.

"A pterodactyl?" Quinn said. "Yes. She'll be in the gym with you."

"Okay, *why* will a pterodactyl be in the gym with us?" Hayden asked.

"Her name is Hisser. She's actually why we're here at the school. We couldn't hold this training anywhere outside. We need a big, enclosed area, like the gym, so she can't fly away. We're trying to get her more accustomed to humans. She won't be interacting with you in any capacity, though. She'll just be in the gym. Don't worry about her."

"I've heard about ignoring the elephant in the room," Gabe said, "but never the pterodactyl in the gym."

"It'll be okay. She calms down when she's out of her cage. And she's well fed. We found her nine months ago. Young. Stranded. Alone. We've been raising her. She's harmless."

"Okay," Gabe said, like he was agreeing, but he wasn't sure if he was.

Walking with the others, Gabe and Hayden entered the gymnasium. The first thing Gabe saw was Hisser's open cage, thirty feet away. There was a leathery flash in the air, an abrupt gust of wind, and then the pterodactyl was perched in the rafters, watching from above, a combination of a bat and a gargoyle. "*So* weird," Gabe murmured, forcing his eyes away from the ancient creature to look around the rest of the gym, where the Wardens' engineers had been busily constructing an obstacle course. There were rope ladders and rope swings. Hurdles. Tunnels. And more.

"This reminds me of those obstacle courses in dog shows," Gabe said. "Well, except for that." He pointed to an animatronic werewolf that was waving its arms while emitting recorded howls. It was one of several arranged around the course, along with similar vampire mannequins, each of them resting on an electrified metal plate. If you got too close, you'd receive a nasty shock.

"So, stay away from the werewolves and vampires?" Joon said. "That's the lesson, here?"

"That's the lesson, here," Quinn agreed.

The two teams studied the course. Gabe did some stretches. Tradd did the same, only a few feet away. They both stared up at Hisser the whole time.

"I didn't expect a pterodactyl today," Tradd said, after a minute.

"Yeah," Gabe agreed. "Although, I suppose that unexpected pterodactyls are about the only types of pterodactyls these days."

"True," Tradd said. Each bit of conversation had a pause between. Gabe wasn't even sure they should be talking to each other. After all, Joon and Tradd were the other team. He concentrated on his stretches. He rolled his neck around from side to side.

"Good work with that mummy," Tradd said, after another pause. "At the Crafters Guild. We saw all the damage. Meeda Obermark told us about the mummy's escape and what you and Hayden did. Nice job."

"Oh, thanks," Gabe said. This little bit of praise—from the other team—made him feel uncomfortable, somehow.

There was no more conversation. Gabe finished his stretches, then rejoined the others. Tradd followed after him and stood by Joon.

"So I'd guess we're competing for the best time?" Gabe asked Quinn Obermark, gesturing to the obstacle course.

"To a certain degree," Quinn answered. "But the important thing is to finish the course without any problems."

"You mean . . . don't get shocked," Tradd said.

"Or get into any fights between your teams," Quinn added.

"Well, I mean, we *are* competing against each other," Joon noted.

"No. Your werewolf and your vampire are competing against each other. You're Trainers, not participants, so don't go joining the battle and start punching each other."

"Of course not," Hayden said, thinking she would do exactly that, if it meant she could keep her medallion.

"Yeah, no way," Tradd said, wondering if he could win a fight against Gabe.

"I'm sure we'll all behave," Joon said while thinking about how if *Hayden* didn't behave, then that girl would find herself in a hornet's nest of trouble.

"I'd like to keep my medallion," Gabe said, the closest one to voicing what they were all feeling.

"Too bad," Tradd told him. "I'm not giving up my medallion. Joon and I spent too much time finding it, and then finding a werewolf. So we're going to beat you."

"It's not like Hayden and I picked up our vampire medallions off the sidewalk," Gabe said. "It took months to find them. And then we had to travel all the way over to Wales. We're not going to just give up, either."

"Wales was beautiful, though," Hayden said.

"Oh, yeah," Gabe agreed. "Incredible country."

"I was there twice," Quinn said. "It really is nice. The first time was a backpacking trip, walking between old castles, camping with my boyfriend of the time. The second time I was meeting Eira Priddy."

"Isn't she . . . ?" Joon asked in amazement.

"The Crafter Witch? In charge of making medallions? Yes. That's her. She's actually quite nice. Very focused on her craft, though. It's a demanding art, with enormous responsibility. But she's also a lot of fun. We went hiking together."

"Why were you meeting Witch Priddy?" Hayden asked.

"Well, how much do you know about the Versus battles?" Quinn asked in turn. They were all standing at the start of the obstacle course. Hayden was trying not to think of the other team, Joon and Tradd, as the enemy, but it wasn't working, so it was best not to think of them at all.

"A lot, I think?" Hayden answered. "But not much, I'd also think."

"Good thinking," Quinn said. "There's a lot that's kept hidden. As you grow older, you'll learn more. As for meeting Witch Priddy, when I was promoted to being a full Warden, I went to Wales to stay with Eira for a week. While I was there, she told me some of the history of the Versus battles, including all about the family who originated them."

"A family started the Versus battles?" Tradd asked. "I don't know anything about that."

"You will. When the time comes. *If* the time comes. We also talked a lot about the reasons behind the battles. The modern world has boxed monsters into a smaller world. The Versus battles help to open that box, a little."

"These medallions come with a lot of responsibility, don't they?" Hayden said. She rolled her vampire medallion around and between her fingers, feeling the weight of it more than ever.

"They come with enormous amounts of responsibility, yes. Count Drustan should hopefully come away from his fight having grown as a vampire. I don't mean he's more powerful; I mean he's a better person. Never lose sight of how monsters have feelings, too. They have dreams. Goals. Just because a vampire is undead doesn't mean you can't make his life better."

"Now I'll feel bad if the werewolf loses," Gabe said, still

keeping an eye on Hisser, above. "A little, anyway. I'd still rather keep my medallion." He noticed Joon and Tradd rolling their eyes.

"Don't feel too bad if the werewolf loses," Quinn said. "What he *reeeeally* wants to do is fight a vampire, and you're giving him the opportunity to do just that. Like I said, these battles are in the nature of monsters. It's part of what *makes* them monsters. And of course you want to keep your medallion. Getting three medallions, winning three battles, means you get your request. Do you already know what you're going to wish for, Gabe? You seem quite motivated."

"Yes," Gabe said. His voice was quiet.

"Oh," Quinn said, noticing the sudden shift in mood. "A secret? That's okay. You don't need to tell me. Or anyone at all. Not yet."

"It's, I guess, not a secret. It's that my uncle, my mom's brother, died of cancer. There were only a few months between him being diagnosed and him being . . . gone."

"Oh," Quinn said. Almost a whisper. "You do know the Wardens and the Crafters, we can't . . . uh, bring anyone back to life? That's not a thing."

"I know. What I want is to become a warlock. It's too late for my uncle, but I *could* protect my parents. Keep them from being taken away. I need to learn magic, and becoming a warlock is the only way to do that."

"Not really," Quinn said. "There are the others." Her expression changed as she spoke, as if she'd surprised herself with what she had said.

"The others?" Gabe asked.

"Nothing," Quinn said, frowning, not meeting Gabe's eyes. "Just a thing I was thinking about. Never mind. Yes, you'd have to be a warlock. That's the only way." The pterodactyl perched in the rafters let out an eerie screech. Everyone ducked. Joon felt a chill go down her back. Her arm hairs stood on end.

"Oh, *crackers*," Hayden said, nervously laughing. "That terrified me."

"I almost screamed," Quinn said, shaking her head. Then she yelled up to the rafters, "Hisser! Seriously? Knock it off." The pterodactyl only preened itself in reply, either ignoring Quinn or acting smug or both.

Quinn turned to Hayden and asked, "What request would you make, if you win enough battles?"

"I'd like to be a witch, similar to how Gabe wants to be a warlock, but my reasons are more selfish. Witches have access to the Crafters Library of Forbidden Books and Forgotten Knowledge. That way, I could not only learn about the secrets of the universe; I could *make* them."

"Whoa," Tradd said.

"Yeah," Gabe agreed. "She gets pretty intense."

"And maybe you're less selfish than you think," Quinn told Hayden. "It sounds to me like you want the opportunities that being a witch can bring. That's fine. It's what you do once you *have* those opportunities that will define you as a person."

"So, what are the rules for the obstacle course?" Hayden

asked. She didn't want to talk about her wish anymore. She didn't want to talk about becoming a witch or an adult. Both of them somehow . . . embarrassed her? That wasn't quite the right word. She felt *something*. Like she was reaching out for something, but didn't know what she was trying to grab. She didn't like other people to see her floundering. She didn't like admitting that the real reason she wanted to win three medallions was that, as a witch, maybe she could somehow bring her parents back together? She'd never even told Gabe the truth of this. Her parents. Back together. It seemed like it would be so simple. She loved them both. They loved each other. It was all right there, in place. So why would it take magic to bring them back together? Hayden didn't want to think about any of it. Not here. Not now. It was best to change the subject.

"The rules?" Quinn said. "Just get through the obstacle course as fast as you can. Both teams run the course at the same time. You can all work together, or you can work separately. Get too close to those werewolf or vampire mannequins, and you *will* get shocked. Get shocked three times, and you're dead."

"Dead?" Tradd asked. Surely the Wardens wouldn't . . . ?

"Not actually *dead*," Quinn explained. "Just disqualified. Well, disqualified and a bit sore. Those shocks *sting*."

"Okay then," Hayden said. "It's just like we said before—stay away from those mannequins."

"What do we win if we're first?" Joon asked.

"Nothing."

"Uh, nothing?" Tradd asked. "What's the point if there's not something to win?"

"Seriously, Tradd?" Quinn said, rolling her eyes. "Do you need a prize to get up in the morning? A trophy to learn something new? To accomplish something you've never done? Sometimes you do things simply because they're there to be done. Not everything comes with cash rewards or fancy certificates."

"Ah," Gabe sighed. "We're learning about life."

"You are," Quinn said, her voice growing stern. "And don't give me that sigh. You're the one who said he wanted to learn magic. You think you're going to learn anything as intricate and elusive as magic if you can't jump a few hurdles? Understand this, the vampire and the werewolf aren't the only ones fighting. The four of you are fighting to learn something new every day, every hour, and every minute. Or at least you *should* be. What you choose to learn comes from your own perspective of the world. If you go through life not paying attention, then life doesn't pay attention to you."

Gabe nodded. It was a lot to take in, and his brain whirled with thoughts he couldn't catch. It felt like a whirlwind inside his head, blowing everything past him. He looked to Joon and Tradd. Maybe it *was* best if they worked together? A combined team? Maybe this wasn't a competition against each other as much as it was all of them—together—against the obstacle course, against the entire world, working as one.

But . . . still. When the *real* fight—the vampire versus the werewolf—happened, one team needed to lose. One team wouldn't get to keep their medallions. His eyes narrowed.

"What's up?" Tradd asked, noticing Gabe's expression, giving him a smile filled with confidence and bravado. "Are you starting to realize your vampire is no match for our werewolf? Is that it? Are you afraid?"

Gabe just looked at Tradd. He thought of working together with him, and he thought of how he'd felt when Count Drustan had risen from his coffin. Those whispering voices and that drumbeat of power in the air. He thought of his uncle, now in a coffin of his own, never to rise again, the cancer that killed him dying along with him. Gabe thought of that mummy, Ptahhotep, and the way his mere existence had shattered the concrete walls of the Crafters Guild. Gabe thought of the werewolf, a beast, but with feelings and emotions of his own. He thought of the medallion in his hand and what it meant if he could keep it. It was his path to becoming a warlock. Gabe thought of what it would be like if his vampire lost in battle against the werewolf. He thought of his golden medallion being taken away. His fingers clenched tighter. He took a long, slow breath.

"Yes, I'm afraid," he told Tradd. "But I'm dealing with it."

CHAPTER 11

"So this is where we're going to fight?" Redd asked, standing with Joon and Tradd on the strangely empty streets of Tacoma, Washington. He waved his hand at the cafés and niche stores and old warehouses converted into apartment buildings.

"This is the place," Joon told the werewolf, who was currently in his human form, looking like a fairly normal, although barefoot man. But as always there was an undercurrent to his humanity, a feeling that the beast might erupt at any time. With Joon watching, gauging his every move, the currently human werewolf strolled past the Fair Pay Pawn Shop, the Little Heaven Ice Cream Emporium, Cat's Rest Book Nook, and more, getting a feel for the neighborhood.

They were alone. Nobody else. Not even when they

strolled through what was known as the Ped Mall, an open walking mall blocked off from all traffic, an area normally bustling with people.

"Where is everyone?" Redd asked as they left the Ped Mall and moved on.

"Gas leak," Tradd said. "They were all evacuated."

Redd sniffed the air, nose held high. "No gas leak," he said, glancing to Tradd.

"No," Tradd said. "That's just the excuse for the evacuation. The people will only be gone a few hours before they get the all clear to return home, but on the night you fight Count Drustan, they'll be evacuated again."

"So this whole playground will be mine," Redd said, reaching out to a brick wall and tracing a finger over the surface. His eyes had gone strange. They reminded Joon of her pet cat Punko's eyes, although Punko's eyes were grayish and pouty, while Redd's eyes were an abyss of incredible darkness, with slashes of red at the edges.

"I'd heard rumors of the Versus, you know," Redd said, vaulting atop a parked car, denting the hood as he landed. "Whispers of the battles. I knew the Versus would find me at some point, or, if not, then I would find it." Down the street, a trio of workers in full hazmat suits had opened a manhole and were—Joon knew—pretending to investigate the gas leak. In reality they were working for the Crafters, watching her and Tradd, and especially the werewolf.

"You can't keep anything secret from a werewolf," Redd

said, sniffing the air. "We smell out everything in time, even the Versus, including those clowns down the street, who think they're in disguise." He pointed to the workers gathered around the open manhole and said, "The tallest had an omelette for breakfast. Red onions and cheddar cheese. Last night he drank grape soda while eating pasta with mushrooms and Parmesan cheese. He uses Maelstrom shaving cream, the one that advertises itself as being for the manliest of men. I could tell you his medical history, which is written in his scent. I could tell you the lives of the people who live in these apartments, and the pets that have walked this sidewalk." He jumped down from the car and sliced a line across the sidewalk with a claw. "I could tell you about every kiss these evacuated residents have had in the last week, how frequently they're doing their laundry, and what detergents they're using. I can smell *everything*. My nose is a giant. Yours is a gnat. A speck." His words were growing more intense. Fur sprouted over his face and from beneath his shirt. He moved closer to Tradd. His mouth elongated. His nostrils flared. The eyes recessed. He was only inches away. A towering beast with incredible menace.

"I've been waiting for the Versus," he said in a rumbling voice, razor-sharp claws sliding out from his fingers. "I could smell it in the air. And I've been waiting for *it* . . . to smell *me*."

The werewolf came closer. Contact. Face-to-face.

"Excuse me," Joon said. The werewolf turned and saw that she was holding up her silver medallion, swaying from its chain.

"Calm down, please," she told him. The werewolf snarled at this, his eyes flickering back and forth between Joon and the medallion in her hand. Then his fur began to recede and his elongated mouth returned to a more human shape, and he gave a long sigh.

"Sorry," he said. "I get irritable. It usually only happens around the full moon. Or a half-moon, to be fair. Sometimes a quarter moon. Honestly, a decent image of a moon on television can get me riled up."

"Sounds . . . bothersome," Joon said, putting her medallion away.

"Nah, I love it." He turned to Tradd and asked, "Mind a few questions?" They were standing in front of the Brindle Auditorium, with its marquee advertising a sold-out show for Sweet Drop, a K-pop band on tour.

"Ask away," Tradd told Redd.

"So, who's out there? Other monsters, I mean."

"Living mummies. Giant women. Minotaurs. Zombies. Ghosts. Lots more. But they have to be kept secret, or there'd be too much chaos in the world."

"Just how big are these giant women?" Redd asked.

Joon said, "They vary in size. Up to almost forty feet. About the height of this auditorium." Together, the three of them looked to the top of the building, four stories above. Redd whistled.

"That's a big woman," he said.

"She lives in Nevada," Joon said. "Her name's Margot. I talked with her last year. She's nice. Terrifying, though."

"Like me," Redd said. "Terrifying, but nice." He nodded to himself. Tradd and Joon shared a silent look.

Redd said, "What I still don't get about this whole thing is . . . why the two of you? What are you? Ten years old?"

"Yes," Tradd said. "We're both ten."

"What do your parents think about all this?" Redd asked.

"My mom's terrified," Joon said. "My dad passed away. Accident at a construction site."

"Oh. Sorry," the werewolf said, his usual grumble softened. "Your mom sounds smart, though." He turned to Tradd and gave a grunt. "Your parents?"

Tradd adjusted his glasses, stalling while he thought about his answer. His mom was a chemical engineer. He often thought of her as a Crafter, except instead of magic she was bending reality by means of science. His dad was a route setter, one of a crew that set up the new climbs at the Face Front Climbing Gym.

"Altogether," Tradd said, "I think you could say they're horrified. Confused. Overwhelmed but supportive."

"So," the werewolf said, looking to both Tradd and Joon. "Your parents *do* know. What I really want to know, though, is . . . why are *you* my Trainers? I'd have expected a squadron of heavily armed soldiers to order me where to go and what to do, but instead of that I'm here in Tacoma with two ten-year-olds holding silver medallions."

Joon said, "Well, the medallions work better against you than any guns."

"Plus, I don't like guns anyway," Tradd said. "People with guns start to believe they need to solve everything with guns, and I think *that's* a monstrous attitude."

"You're not answering my real question," the werewolf growled.

"People with fangs tend to think they can solve everything with fangs," Tradd muttered, then, louder, said, "You mean about us being ten years old?" The werewolf nodded.

"People our age think more about the future and less about the past," Joon said. "Which means we come in with open minds. We don't judge people like you, you specifically, by what *other* werewolves have done in the past. We judge you as a person rather than a monster."

"I'm not really a person anymore, though," Redd said. "I'm much closer to a monster." He showed his fangs to make his point, and then let out a howl that sent pigeons fluttering into the air and squirrels scrambling for cover.

"Show-off," Tradd told Redd. "But I can probably belch louder than that. Listen, you don't have to try to scare us. Believe me, we're scared. We know you're a monster, but I can tell you still have a lot of human in you. Like that forest you made? It must've been an incredible amount of work to raise trees in a warehouse. To bring in all that soil? Amazing."

"And that moon you made?" Joon added. "The railroad tracks in the rafters? You're an artist! I mean, sure, Tradd and I know you're powerful enough to challenge an actual literal vampire in a fight, but anyone who could build an authentic forest? *That's* a real accomplishment."

"I'm strong enough to do a lot more than just challenge a vampire," Redd said with menace, like he was not only prepared to fight a vampire, but also any children who questioned his ability to win.

"I'd really love to have a forest like that," Joon said, waving off Redd's comment. "My own little place where I could escape. Some deer would be nice. Although I suppose there's the whole question of them going to the bathroom all over my forest."

"Deer are total slobs," Redd agreed. "You think they're pretty and gentle, which I suppose they are, but they're absolutely not known for cleaning up after themselves, and they chew just, like, . . . everything. I tried to add other animals to my forest. I mean, I do have birds and squirrels, and of course I needed to—what's the best word?—*install* a bunch of insects in order to keep nature working the way she needs to, but any larger animals are harder. I'm still working on it."

"Why not live in an actual forest?" Tradd asked. They were taking seats at one of the outdoor tables at the Stockings Café. There was a water station, where Tradd got glasses of water for everyone. Redd put up his feet on an empty chair next to Tradd and began picking at his toes, toes that did not—in Tradd's estimation—either look or smell the best, but of course you made allowances when you were hanging out with a werewolf.

Finally, wiping something off his left foot with a napkin

yanked from a dispenser, Redd answered, "I'd rather live in a real forest, to be honest. An entire forest. I could run for hours and be miles and miles from where I began, instead of just circling back to where I started, the way I do in January Memorial Forest."

"January Memorial Forest?" Joon asked. "That's the name of your forest?"

"It is. Partially named after the month when I started building it, but mostly it's named after my mom. She died when I was a teen. A heart attack."

"Sorry to hear that, Redd," Tradd told the werewolf.

"It got lonely after that," Redd said, nodding to Tradd. "I did try to live in a forest, but there was always hikers and a few hunters, and I couldn't stop thinking of them as trespassers on my land."

"You didn't hurt any of them, did you?" Joon asked.

"So after a time I understood I needed a forest of my own," Redd said, ignoring Joon's question, which she decided against repeating. "My mom was good with plants. She taught me a lot. So I built a forest, and I watched online tutorials whenever I needed to build something. I've always been good with my hands. And I can smell whenever something is going wrong. If a plant isn't getting the right nourishment, I can sniff out the problem. Literally."

"Maybe you could open your own landscaping company?" Joon said.

"Nah, I don't have a lot of patience for people. Frankly, if you kids weren't only ten years old, I'd have a lot less patience with you. You'd say something wrong and I'd be a werewolf in the blink of an eye, and then we'd see if you were . . . oh."

"Oh?" Tradd asked.

"I just realized. That's another reason you kids are watching over me. I don't see you as a threat. I won't immediately fight you. I'm going to listen to what you have to say."

"Exactly," Joon said. "Kids are smarter."

"That's . . . not exactly what I said. Or meant. But let's stick with that. And, if I'm going to listen to what a pair of kids have to say, then say something. Tell me when the fight is supposed to happen. Tell me the rules."

"The fight is four days from now," Tradd said. "Starting at midnight. We figured both you and Count Drustan would like that."

"I would like that," Redd agreed. He picked up the napkin dispenser and lobbed it at a trio of pigeons. They scattered, taking flight. Then they quickly landed again, gathering around the napkin dispenser to peck at it, checking to see if it was food.

"As far as the rules for the Versus battles, you're not allowed to leave this designated area," Joon said, waving her hand to the surrounding blocks, "but the main rule is that you're not allowed to kill each other."

"Hmmp," Redd grunted in disgust, watching as Tradd retrieved the napkin dispenser and—after using one of its napkins to wipe it clean—returned it to the table. Redd picked it up and tossed it again, this time farther out at a different group of pigeons. They too scattered. And they too returned to investigate the dispenser.

"What are the other rules?" Redd asked. "Besides not escaping off into the night, and this annoying rule about leaving that vampire alive?"

"No other rules," Tradd said, returning with the napkin dispenser again, wiping it clean and replacing it on the table, this time keeping a hand on top of it, casually pinning it down.

"No other rules?" Redd asked.

"Would you *follow* any other rules?" Joon asked.

"I might not follow the rules you already told me," Redd admitted.

"Which is why there aren't any other rules."

"Smart. So, what can you tell me about this bloodsucker I'll be fighting?"

"He's a vampire," Tradd said. "Quite old, and vampires grow stronger over time, so he's very powerful. He ruled a huge swath of Wales several hundred years ago, keeping everyone terrified of his power."

"Yeah, that's definitely a vampire thing."

"Let's see," Tradd said, thinking of all the research he and Joon had done on the vampire Redd needed to fight. "He sided with some guy named Owain Glyndŵr in a battle for Welsh independence from the English, but it didn't work out, and he ended up sealed away in his own castle. That was in, um . . ." Tradd trailed off and looked to Joon.

"Back in 1413," she said. "Over six hundred years ago. Count Drustan missed a *lot* of birthday parties packed away in that coffin of his."

"All fascinating," Redd said. "But I meant, tell me about his personality. His specific powers?"

"We're not sure. And Gabe Basuldua and Hayden Fracasso—they're the Trainers in charge of Count Drustan—aren't spilling the beans on this one. So, we're assuming Drustan has all the usual abilities. He can likely transform into mist. Or ravens or bats or wolves. Maybe other things? And he can probably command the minds of lesser beings. Rats and cats and mice and maybe a lot more."

"Lesser beings like . . . humans?" Redd asked.

"Funny," Joon said, meaning the opposite. "Also kinda mean. But yeah, maybe he can. Maybe he can control your mind, too, so watch for that. As far as his personality, it's rather forceful from what we're hearing, which isn't a surprise."

"Yeah," Redd said. "That's another vampire thing."

"If he's anything like other vampires," Tradd said, "then he heals whenever he transforms. It helps restore him from any injuries. Of course, blood heals him even faster. And he's undoubtedly super strong and blindingly fast."

"We'll see," Redd said. He didn't seem worried.

Joon said, "We have reports he's enjoying the modern world. New technologies. New cultures. New cuisines."

"New people to dine on," Redd said. "That's another vampire thing." He brushed Tradd's hand aside from the napkin dispenser and was about to toss it at the pigeons again.

"Can you quit that, please?" Tradd asked.

"No," Redd said, and tossed it. It thumped to the sidewalk and bumped into a pigeon, which squalled in annoyance and gave the napkin dispenser a vigorous revenge peck. Glaring at Redd, Tradd picked up the dispenser for a third time and once more returned it to the table.

"Don't do that again," Tradd said.

"You didn't say 'please' this time," Redd noted, reaching for the scuffed dispenser.

"It didn't work the first time," Tradd said with a shrug, reaching into his pocket to bring out his medallion. "But maybe *this* will." Redd saw what Tradd was doing and began subtly changing, a little more fur, a little more fang, a little more wolf, and a lot more muscle. By the time Tradd had his medallion out, Redd was half man, half werewolf, and entirely terrifying. Even the nearby pigeons, as unwise as they were, moved farther back. Redd leaned in closer, his eyes gone black with menace, a scent like iron and rotting tobacco, his nails—his claws—scratching at the table as he leaned ever closer to the ten-year-old Tradd.

"Put that away, little boy," the werewolf ordered, his words sharp.

"Nope," Tradd said, meeting the werewolf's dark eyes while placing his silver medallion atop the napkin dispenser, using two fingers to hold it in place, the chain slipping off the edge.

Redd, almost totally in werewolf form, stared at the medallion. A prickling of his flesh sent his thick hair flowing like a field of fetid wheat. His eyes closed for a moment, then opened, looking at Tradd and looking to Joon, who was now holding up her own medallion.

"Those infuriating things," Redd snarled, although in almost good-natured fashion.

"Even you, Redd, can't fight against a medallion," Tradd said, putting his medallion away as Redd regained his human form.

"Maybe not," Redd said, leaning back in his chair. "But I *can* fight against a vampire, and it's going to be great."

CHAPTER 12

Count Drustan walked out of Gentlemen's Best Clothiers in a three-piece tweed check suit, enjoying the feel of the cloth and the sharp tappings of his hard heels on the bricks beneath his feet. Night was falling. He was walking in the Pedestrian Mall, the Ped Mall, a cross section of brick-lined streets blocked off from all traffic, the home to niche stores and cafés and restaurants and more. It was two days after the evacuation for the "gas leak," and the crowds had returned in full, with office workers stopping off for drinks on the way home and a mix of partiers already out for the evening. Three women, students from the nearby University of Puget Sound, were discussing a professor of theirs and how well she dressed, her bobbed hair and cashmere sweaters. As Count Drustan walked past the women, their voices slid into whispers they thought nobody else could hear, and perhaps that would have been true, except for any nearby vampire.

"Talk about well-dressed," a brunette woman said, in breathy, complimentary tones.

"More men should wear suits," a woman in a red sweater declared.

"Are those kids *with* him?" the last woman asked. She had the best smile of the three, which was why she'd thought Count Drustan had given her in particular a brief smile, a companionable nod to a fellow member of the Good Smile Club, and she would never know that the reason he'd smiled at her was because of her white T-shirt with "BITE" in red letters.

The women began discussing Gabe and Hayden, two children who the women decided *must* be adopted, since they didn't look anything like Count Drustan, and maybe that meant he was single, an uncle or something, and would he like to grab a drink after he dropped off the children with their real parents? Their whimsical conversation continued, but Count Drustan let his attention stray from the women and on to the children with him. Two nine-year-olds. How strange. In his day, children were terrified of him, but these two were obviously enjoying this outing, this quest to update both his clothing and his understanding of this world in which he'd awoken.

"How do I look?" he asked the children, displaying his new suit.

"Not bad," Hayden said, glad the Crafters Guild was

paying for everything, since she'd seen the prices on the suits. "You look less like a cheesy 1960s horror film actor, now." She watched Drustan's eyes, seeing him digest the comment. He'd learned about movies and films, but it still took a moment for him to understand the reference.

"You look like a college professor," Gabe said. "Probably history classes. Or math."

"I *could* teach a lot about history," Drustan said. "At least certain parts of it. I'm a little lax on anything that's happened in the last six hundred years." He was watching the throats of a couple in their forties, two men walking together, both of them in Real Madrid soccer jerseys. He was also watching the throat of a man drumming on the bottoms of several plastic buckets, a street musician playing for tips, and he was watching the throats of a man and a woman kissing their goodbyes to each other, standing in front of a stairway leading up to the second-floor apartments above the Ring-A-Bell Deli. The vampire could feel the rise of their heartbeats, the excitement in their pulses, the steaming *charge* of blood through their veins, whispering to him with a voice he could hear and an allure he could barely resist.

"Stop staring at everyone's throats," Hayden said, tapping her medallion on the side of his arm, bringing him out of his reverie. "It's rude."

"Old habits are hard to break," Count Drustan said. "Especially when they're delicious. But I wonder, where did you get those medallions? You say the Wardens didn't give them to you?"

"We have to find them ourselves," Gabe said. "It's part of the test. The Wardens don't want just any random seven-year-old—that's the youngest a Trainer can be—to take charge of a dinosaur, or anything like that. Finding the medallions is part of what qualifies us to take part."

"And where does one look for medallions?" Count Drustan asked. "I take it they're not available for sale in any of the local markets?"

"No," Hayden said. "They're often found in archaeological digs. Old tombs. Ancient libraries uncovered behind hidden doorways, or secret rooms in churches that have stood for centuries. I *have* noticed a couple online, though, for sale on auction sites. Less dramatic, but still nice to have." She dug around in her pocket and pulled out a medallion made of sandstone. The features were indistinct. Weathered. "I'm not even sure what this one is. I've spent *countless* hours in libraries, trying to pin it down. Maybe it's a griffin? Not sure."

"Let me see," the vampire said, holding out his hand. Hayden hesitated, shuffling her feet on the bricks of the Ped Mall, and then handed it over. The vampire rolled it around in his fingers, touching the stone surface, with the medallion's fine iron chain slithering about in snakelike fashion as he studied the well-preserved "V" on the back and the much-weathered creature depicted on the front. It was clearly a beast of some kind. Hayden sometimes believed it was a lion, but that didn't make sense, because nothing as commonplace as a lion would ever take part in a Versus battle.

"It's a sphinx," Drustan said.

"What?" Hayden blurted. "A sphinx? Really? How do you know?"

"These lines at the edges," the vampire said, pointing. "Did you think these were just scratches?"

"Well, yes," Hayden admitted.

"They're not. They're as badly weathered as the sphinx, but this is Hittite lettering."

"Hittite?" Gabe asked. He remembered that the Hittites were ancient, their language and culture largely vanishing well over three thousand years ago. "You can read Hittite?"

"I can read most languages," the vampire said. "Well, most of them from my time, and times previous. This medallion even names the sphinx in particular. Kasku. That's a Hittite name, incidentally. The full inscription reads, 'Kasku in wisdom bathes, but the droplets he leaves are dark.'"

"That sounds weird," Gabe said. "And ominous."

"I have a sphinx medallion, though!" Hayden said, grinning at the vampire, who gave her a soft smile in return. "Now I can hunt a sphinx!"

"How do you hunt?" Count Drustan asked, handing back the medallion. "How did you find me?"

"Endless research," Gabe said. "The Wardens have

enormous libraries. We found the first mention of you in the Voynich Manuscript, a series of writings from the fifteenth century, largely centered on plant life, but one of the plants is named Stopblood Garlic, a variant of crow garlic that can ward off vampires and was said to have been used to ward off *you* in particular, stopping you from attacking a milliner's wife, Quenilda Parrock."

"Oh, *her*?" the vampire laughed. "That's rubbish. She didn't ward me off with garlic. She warded me off by being a thoroughly unpleasant woman."

"I'll make a note," Hayden promised. "The point is, now that we had some idea of where you were at, geographically, we were able to zero in on other references, including in *The Triumphs of Man O'er Nature Untoward*, a handwritten book from the sixteenth century of which there's only one copy known, and which chronicles various tales of men defeating monsters. Not that, uh, you're a monster."

"We're all monsters," the vampire said. "You'll learn that if you reach the age of two hundred. Hopefully we're not all as monstrous as that jester there, though."

"Jester?" Gabe asked. Count Drustan was gazing toward a man strumming on a guitar, wanting to join the musician playing the bucket drums, although the man on the drums was waving him away, which Gabe could well understand, since the drummer was talented and the guitar player was, to be kind, not.

"That jester on the strange lute," Count Drustan said. "He offends my ears. And so, he pays the price." Hearing the threat in the vampire's voice, Gabe tightened his grip on his medallion, worried the vampire was on the attack, but Count Drustan was instead staring intently at . . . pigeons? A small gathering of pigeons was nearby, pecking at this and that, but suddenly they all turned and stared at the guitar player, who was now serenading a couple, obviously hoping to earn a little coin, but it was clear that he was just bothering them.

And then the pigeons attacked. The whole group took flight, soaring straight for the guitar player, fluttering and pecking at him while emitting the angriest coos Gabe had ever heard. The guitar player was forced to retreat, scurrying across the Ped Mall holding his guitar over his head for the scant protection it provided, with the pigeons flapping after him on the attack.

Gabe asked the vampire, "Did . . . you just take over the minds of those pigeons in order to attack the guitar player?"

"Absolutely yes."

"Oh," Gabe said. "Well. Hmm. Don't do that." The vampire said nothing in reply. The three of them stood in silence.

Then Hayden said, "He really *was* annoying, though, wasn't he? That guitar guy?"

"He was," Gabe admitted.

The vampire still said nothing. But his silence was notably smug.

CHAPTER 13

"He's ready," Hayden told Meeda Obermark, the Crafter in charge of the training exercise. Meeda was once more wearing a red suit, and once more accompanied by Quinn, currently dressed in yellow slacks with a bumblebee-patterned blouse. They stood with Gabe Basuldua, Hayden's nine-year-old friend and teammate, and Count Maenwallon Drustan, their seven-hundred-year-old vampire.

They were on Fox Island, situated in the Puget Sound near Tacoma, Washington, standing on the edges of what was known as Camp Falsehood, an elaborate outdoor training facility constructed to look like a section of Tacoma itself, three blocks in all. It had originally been built to host Versus battles, but real towns were preferred now, since it was strange to attempt to integrate monsters into society but then use a fake city.

Camp Falsehood was made up of warehouses that would never be used. Apartment buildings where no one would ever live and cafés where no one would ever eat. The current "population" included twenty-seven werewolves made of wax, wood, and straw, and the goal of the training exercise was simple: Count Drustan needed to hunt these imitation werewolves and utterly destroy them. He had thirty minutes.

"Let me check my team," Meeda told Hayden. She walked a few steps off and took out her phone. Gabe half listened as she contacted a wide range of people. The ones in charge of activating the werewolf dummies, making them move in robotic fashion. The technicians responsible for replicating the horrible werewolf howls and equally terrible musky scents. She talked to the construction engineers who'd built the replica buildings, and the camera operators who would film the exercise.

Hayden, meanwhile, stared at the vampire. It was... exciting. She was about to see him in action, at last. Her mind flashed back to *Red Teeth*, a comic book series about vampires that her mother had illustrated. The vampires had been unstoppable. The comics had been terrifying. Her mother was very talented at illustrating the shadows, the teeth, the eyes, the blood.

"How are you feeling?" Quinn asked Count Drustan.

"Alive," the vampire said. "And full."

"Well, you're not really alive," Quinn said. "But I'm not surprised you're full." She gestured to a small pile of blood packets, ten in all. Ten *empty* packets, to be more precise.

"I do enjoy a hearty meal," the vampire said. His words came out throaty, which was fitting, since he was staring at Quinn's throat, as if hungry for more. Hayden nudged him and told him to behave.

"The sun's not bothering you?" Quinn asked. The skies were cloudy, but the clouds were white and bright and the sun was intermittently in full view, shining enthusiastically down from above.

"I won't say it's pleasant," the vampire said. "But I'm old enough to endure it with a fair amount of ease. No worries of me being incinerated, if that's what you're asking."

"It's a beautiful view," Quinn said, looking to the waters of the Puget Sound and the towering whiteness of Mount Rainier in the distance, like a ghost on the horizon.

"Beautiful indeed," the vampire said, looking to the blue veins in Quinn's white throat.

Hayden poked Count Drustan in the side and whispered, "Stop it. You're embarrassing me."

"Count Drustan," Meeda called out from twenty feet in the distance, looking to the vampire with curious eyes. "Are you doing something?"

"He's just hungry," Hayden told the Warden. "*Still* hungry. Somehow. But it's okay. I'm handling it."

"That's not what I meant," Meeda said. She pointed to her phone and said, "I'm being told there's . . . rats? And mice? Plus a rather impressive number of crows. They seem to be searching out the werewolves? Apparently, one of the wax werewolves is absolutely *covered* with flies. Is this you, Drustan?"

"There are no rules against me coercing a few friends to my cause, are there?" the vampire said in reply. The tone of his voice suggested that it was ridiculous to give him any rules at all. Hayden could hear the vampire's voice whispering in her mind. It felt warm. Like a trickle of water seeping into her thoughts, whispering things. She clutched tighter at her medallion and moved a few steps back from the monster.

"No rules at all," Meeda said. "And quit trying to bully about in my mind. It's enough of a mess in there without you cluttering things up." She turned back to her phone. The vampire emitted a low chuckle, obviously amused at the impertinence.

"It's him," Meeda told someone, speaking into her phone. Then she put her phone away and said, "Everyone's ready. You're good to go."

"I'm gone," the vampire said. And he was. Hayden saw nothing but a puff of movement. A flash of mist. The merest possibility of a raven she might only have imagined.

Meeda's phone buzzed.

"Yes?" she answered, listening to someone on her phone, but looking to Quinn, and to Gabe, and to Hayden. She nodded several times, listening, then relayed the news.

"The werewolf dummies," she said. "They're all basically exploding."

CHAPTER 14

Hours after the vampire had left, Joon and Tradd stood with Carter Addo—one of the regional captains of the Wardens—on a balcony overlooking a street in Camp Falsehood. Together, they munched on the chocolate chip cookies Joon had baked, which Carter mentioned were so full of butter that he worried they'd melt in the sun. He clearly loved them, though. Joon noticed him sliding a few into his pocket.

Down below, in the street, a werewolf was hunting. Sort of. Mostly he was just . . . standing still?

"What's he doing?" Carter asked.

"Not sure," Joon said. She leaned over the railing and called out, "Hey, Redd! What are you doing?" The werewolf didn't answer or even look in Joon's direction. He was just standing still, head held high, sniffing.

"He's only got five minutes left," Carter said.

"How many of the fake vampires has he taken down?" Tradd asked.

"None, according to my people. He *has* come near a few of them, and *definitely* noticed them, but he doesn't seem interested? You explained this training session to him, right?"

"Thought so," Joon said. The werewolf was loping off. There was one of the fake vampires in a little alcove, one of the many targets Redd was supposed to destroy, but he barely glanced at it, being more interested in sniffing at a nearby wall. A howl burst from his throat, sending shivers up and down Joon's spine. It was the sound of the hunt. A primal sound. Birds scattered from their perches on the empty buildings of Camp Falsehood. A deer broke from hiding and bounded off down the street, skidding when it took a corner. The werewolf scaled the side of the building, claws digging into the wood, scampering up the outer wall as sure as a squirrel on a tree. In seconds he'd reached the roof and stood sniffing the air, three stories above the street. There was another of the fake vampires near him on the roof. Joon thought the werewolf would destroy it, but he ignored the wax-and-wood vampire completely, strolling past it and then picking up speed, running for the edge of the roof.

"He's . . . jumping?" Carter whispered, just as Redd reached the edge of the roof and leapt off. It was a leap beyond all reason, fifty feet across the void, from one building to another. It was an impossible jump that the werewolf made easily, landing softly one building over and one story up from where Joon and Tradd were watching with Carter. Soon, the beast was out of sight.

"Good legs," Joon said.

"Incredible legs," Carter agreed. "But, he only has three minutes left and hasn't destroyed a single vampire. Did his animal mind understand the purpose of this exercise?"

"Yes," a voice full of gravel answered, just as a wave of fetid odor washed over them from behind.

The werewolf was there. Behind them. Looming over them. A monster in size and nature. The werewolf's fur tickled the back of Joon's neck before she turned, reflexively bringing up her medallion to ward away the creature.

"Ooo," the werewolf said, in mocking tones. "There's your pretty medallion again. Guess I'll do what you ask, as long as you're asking me to fight vampires. That's what I'm doing, you know."

Carter said, "Then why weren't you—?"

"Destroying wax dummies? Why would I? I don't need to play with dolls. What I've been doing instead is hunting the scent of that vampire. The actual one. His scent is . . . fascinating. He moves quicker than I would have thought. And, differently. I can tell whenever he turned into a raven. The scent of those feathers. The linger of his dead flesh in the air. He's harder to track whenever he turned to smoke. It took some concentration. A question, though. Who was it that put *my* supposed scent on the werewolf dummies? I can still catch it in the air. It's ludicrous. The scent wasn't even close. No, wait. Don't tell me who it was. I don't need a name. I have her scent. I'll find her." He leapt off the balcony, landed easily, and began loping off.

"Don't hurt anyone!" Joon called out from above.

"*Seriously?*" the werewolf called back in disbelief.

"Seriously," Joon said. She could hear the werewolf's disgusted exhale and see the droop of his shoulders. He stood still for long moments. Then he turned and walked back, suddenly leaping two floors up, landing on the balcony so close to Tradd that he was knocked back, and so close to Carter that the Warden fell to the floor beneath the towering monster.

"Don't hurt anyone," the werewolf mocked, his voice raw and snarling. Tradd tried to pull the werewolf away from Carter, but it was like tugging at a wall. The creature remained looming over the fallen Warden, his teeth bared and his dark eyes lined with red.

"Don't hurt anyone," the werewolf said again, disgusted. "You hold your medallions and make demands. You shout your orders, trying to hold back my teeth." It was difficult for Tradd to understand the beast's words. They were too filled with rage and howls and with something utterly inhuman, a mockery of a human voice.

"But there is a price for all things," the werewolf snarled. "Nature demands payment. Nature demands balance." His massive head lowered closer and closer to Carter. Tradd could hear voices, shouted orders from the Wardens' guards, the keen odor of electricity in the air as shock weapons were readied, the smell of ozone mixing with the deeply humid stench of the werewolf.

"Nature demands to be fed," the werewolf said, his teeth inches from Carter's skull. "Nature wants to chew. Nature wants *meat*."

Guards were trying to rush onto the balcony, but there was no room. The werewolf filled the space. It felt like he filled the world.

The werewolf, crouched over the fallen Warden, stepped back and then stood. The massive beast looked down to Carter for one heartbeat, then another, and then he put out his hand as if to help Carter up. Joon could see the hesitancy on the Warden's face, but Carter made a decision and slowly, tentatively, put out his hand for the beast. The werewolf took his hand and helped him up.

"Nature wants balance," the werewolf said. "But it doesn't *need* to be meat. It *could* be those last three chocolate chip cookies I smell in your pocket." One huge hand reached out, a finger extended, and tap-tapped at the left pocket of Carter's suit jacket.

"Oh," Carter said in a breathless voice. "Oh. Yes. Okay. That would be fine."

CHAPTER 15

Gabe looked in his hotel room's mirror, wondering what to wear tomorrow, the day of battle. It would take place at night, but the weather was supposed to be warm. The skies, cloudless. "Just a shirt," he told his reflection. "Pants. Shoes. Everything is normal." He watched his reflection mouth the words. *Everything is normal.* But it wasn't. Tomorrow was the fight. Gabe watched his reflection, the way he was breathing too fast. He closed his eyes. Tomorrow was the fight.

Hayden sat in the movie theater. The air felt cold. The movie was from the 1950s. A musical. Eating popcorn with so much salt her tongue was stinging, she watched the dances. The men and women twirling. Voices singing. She'd gone to the theater alone, and if anyone had sat next to her and asked what she was watching, she couldn't have told them. Her mind was entirely elsewhere.

"Tomorrow," she whispered, so low that nobody could have heard her, not over the sound of the music.

Joon sat to the rear of a café, looking up pictures of werewolves on the internet. Nothing captured the reality of the werewolf. The horrifying power of his presence. The smell. The menace. That primal voice. Joon drank too much soda. Ate too many donuts. Her heart was racing.

"Tomorrow," she said, clicking through images.

Tradd had his phone on the café table, next to a croissant. His medallion was there, too, with the silver chain encircling his phone and its image of Keeper, his lost dog.

"Tomorrow," Tradd told his medallion.

"Tomorrow," he promised Keeper.

Count Drustan turned to a raven and sat perched on the back of the couch in the cabin on the shore of Lake Chelan. His feathers ruffled. He let his mind expand to feel the nearest animals in the forest, the squirrels and deer and others. They had little concept of time, these creatures.

Regardless, the whispers in their minds held them fascinated. Tomorrow. Tomorrow. *Tomorrow*.

Redd woke from a dream. He remembered a chase through city streets. Blood everywhere. Terrified screams. Fangs growing from walls. Something roaring. All that blood.

"A good dream," he murmured, and went back to sleep.

CHAPTER 16

The surrounding blocks were empty. All the apartments. All the stores. Evacuated. Everyone who lived in this Tacoma neighborhood had been moved to hotels. Everyone who worked here had been sent back to their homes, far outside the radius of where the vampire would fight a werewolf. The people hadn't been told, of course. The cover story was a second gas leak, far worse than the first. Old pipes. Poorly installed. The city was working on it. Helicopters patrolled the skies, not only warding off the airspace, but also carrying Wardens to monitor the fight and provide aid if needed. Computer experts had shut down all security cameras. The streets were blocked by dark cars driven by men and women in dark suits, constantly talking on jet-black phones. There were no unauthorized eyes of any sort.

Gabe and Hayden stood at one end of this oddball arena,

this cleared section of Tacoma, Washington. Joon and Tradd were at the other end, seven blocks away. Hayden and Gabe were next to the Soft More Ice Cream Factory. Tradd and Joon stood in the street between the 506 Plumbers Union Building and the Donny Brook Tattoo Parlor.

Gabe and Hayden had a vampire.

Joon and Tradd had a werewolf.

And tonight, they were going to fight.

It was dark, almost midnight. A gray cat watched from the steps of the union building, staring at the werewolf. A beagle, left behind in the rush of the evacuation, sat in the sheltered doorway of the ice cream store, growling low at the vampire from a distance he clearly didn't want to narrow.

The vampire had his fangs in view.

The werewolf had his claws out.

The moon was full overhead, though clouds were gathering, threatening to obscure the view. Both the vampire and the werewolf—still blocks apart from each other at this point—looked to the moon and smiled.

"Three minutes to go," Tradd said. The werewolf was pacing back and forth, brimming with power, muscles flexing.

"Two minutes to go," Hayden said, not long after, but several blocks away. The vampire was like a statue beside her. But he radiated confidence. And menace. He felt like an abyss that wanted to pull her within.

"One minute to go," Joon and Tradd told the werewolf, looking at their phones and echoing the same words Gabe and Hayden were telling Count Drustan. The moon seemed to grow even more full, as if drawing an enormous breath in expectation.

"Time," Joon said, even as a bell began to ring out across the empty blocks, shattering the silence of the night. Even before the first echoes, the werewolf was in motion, speeding down the evacuated street and exploding in through the front window of the Positively Pages bookstore, shredding books as he disappeared into the darkness within. Only seconds later there was a tremendous rumble and the store next door—Hugh's High Fashions—had a headless mannequin crash out through the front window and bounce halfway across the street, one arm breaking away amid the cascade of shattering glass. The big bell continued ringing, but otherwise the street went silent.

"Time," Gabe said as the first tollings of the bell swept over the buildings and echoed in the night. The vampire stood motionless beside him. He hadn't even blinked.

"Time," Gabe repeated. Had the vampire heard? It was difficult to tell from Count Drustan's expression. He seemed lost in thought. Focused elsewhere.

"Time," Hayden told the vampire, echoing Gabe's words much as the bell was echoing its tolls. Even from across town, they could hear the werewolf's destruction had already begun. She chanced a tiny nudge in the vampire's side, wanting to bring him out of his reverie. But it was like poking stone.

A cat meowed from behind a hedge, then walked out into the street.

"Kitty, what are you doing here?" Hayden said. "You should probably find cover. There's going to be—" But that was as far as she got before another cat emerged from an alley, and another leapt down from a windowsill to the street. These cats were joined by others, all of them silent except for that first meow, a collection of twenty cats gathering in the deserted street. Soon, pigeons began to land among them, floating noiselessly down from the rooftops, abandoning their nighttime roosts. Together, the pigeons and cats gazed to the north, the south, the east and west, and to the buildings above.

The pigeons took sudden flight, speeding into the air and spreading out into the night. The cats hissed and ran off in all directions, their eyes scanning the streets and the shadows.

"It's time," Count Drustan said, and began walking.

CHAPTER 17

"This way," Joon said, looking at the location tracker on her phone. With it, she could see the exact locations of not only herself and Tradd, but of Gabe, Hayden, and Redd as well. She had no way to track Count Drustan, unfortunately. His location was a mystery.

Three cats raced by. The last momentarily slowed to hiss at Joon, but then was gone with the others, disappearing into the darkness of an alley.

"Weird," Joon muttered, returning her attention to her phone, where she was tracking Gabe and Hayden. Maybe the vampire was with them? If so, she could call Redd and alert him to his opponent's location. Not that Joon really believed he'd answer his phone. The werewolf had scoffed at her when she—an hour earlier—had given him the phone and told him that, if she could, she'd find out where the vampire was at and tell him.

"I don't need a phone," he'd laughed. "I have my nose." Well, that was great for a werewolf, but Joon wasn't a werewolf. She was a ten-year-old girl who loved going for walks around her hometown of Roanoke and petting all the dogs she saw. She loved renting karaoke machines with her friends and belting out songs by Taylor Swift and Blackpink, and Disney songs that had—over the last years—devolved into slightly improper alternative lyrics. Her nose wasn't made for sniffing vampires.

A small flock of pigeons swept low over Joon, making her gasp. Tradd began joking about how there were actual werewolves and vampires in the night, but it was *pigeons* that scared Joon, when the pigeons curved in midflight and dive-bombed him, missing him only because he dove for the sidewalk, with his glasses knocked askew and his phone clattering across the concrete. The pigeons landed next to him, and, before he could react, one pecked at his forehead. Then the birds all took flight and flapped away into the darkness.

"What the heck was *that*?" Tradd asked, still sprawled on the concrete. A hamburger wrapper floated past him down the sidewalk, swept along by a rising wind.

"Those birds were strange," Joon said, helping Tradd to his feet. "Like, *everything* is looking for a fight tonight."

"Please don't tell anyone I got into a fight with pigeons and lost," Tradd said, retrieving his phone. Then a terrible howling cut through the night. Clouds slid in front of the moon, plunging the night into deeper darkness.

"That way?" Tradd said, pointing in the direction of the walking mall.

"Yes," Joon said, checking her phone, watching a red dot moving at impressive speed across the map on her display.

"He's only a block from Gabe and Hayden," Tradd said, looking at his own map. A wet maple leaf stuck to his shirt. He pulled it off and flicked it aside. The wind sent it right back at him.

"You have both your medallions, right?" Joon asked. Tradd understood her worry. Thinking of how close the werewolf was to the other Trainers made Joon consider how close Count Drustan—the vampire—might be to *them*. Luckily, they did have some defense. Two hours ago, the Wardens had issued them vampire medallions to go along with their werewolf medallions. Their vampire medallions weren't as strong as Gabe's and Hayden's, but they'd at least provide some level of protection.

"Got it," Tradd said, holding up his vampire medallion, which clinked against his werewolf one, the two of them swinging from their chains. Hopefully, not long from now, he'd be able to officially keep his werewolf medallion, making him one step closer to finding his dog, Keeper, and bringing him home. He could picture the terrier sleeping on a pile of blankets at the foot of Tradd's bed, or chasing squirrels in the park, full of joy at the chase.

"Let's try to catch up with Redd," Joon said, hurrying

down the street, looking at the red dot on her phone. The werewolf, now in the area of the Pedestrian Mall, wasn't moving anymore. Maybe he'd found the vampire? Maybe they were already fighting? She and Tradd had to get there, fast.

"Cats," Tradd said.

"Cats?" Joon asked, but she already saw what he was talking about. There were several cats racing along with them, and then the cats sped ahead even as a flock—a veritable swarm—of pigeons flew past, with all the cats and pigeons heading in the same direction as she and Tradd were running. Something was *definitely* happening in the Pedestrian Mall ahead. Joon could hear crashing noises. Shattering glass. Heavy impacts.

And howls.

Ten minutes earlier, Hayden and Gabe watched their vampire turn to smoke. There was a noise like the softest of coughs, then nothing but a hazy column of smoke where the vampire had been. The smoke acted odd, not dispersing, but instead collecting together, slithering away through the air. Soon it was gone.

"You have his location on your phone?" Hayden asked, looking to her own phone.

"No. I've got nothing," Gabe answered.

"Me either. Maybe he doesn't register when he turns to smoke?" She hadn't considered what the tracking device would do when Count Drustan transformed. After all, when the vampire turned to smoke, his clothing transformed, too. Why would the tracking device be any different? But just because it wasn't any different didn't mean it would *work*. Hayden had to hope the tracker would regain solid—*working*—form whenever Count Drustan changed back.

"There!" Gabe said, looking at his phone. "I've got him again! He's . . . up there?" He looked up to the Altitude Climbing Gym, an old theater only recently restored as a gym. Count Drustan was standing atop the three-story building, gazing out over the street, backlit by the moon and clouds.

Relieved to see that her tracker was again registering the vampire's location, Hayden glanced up to him just in time to see Count Drustan step off the edge and begin plummeting to the sidewalk.

"Ahh!" she shrieked, but before the vampire had fallen more than a few feet, he transformed into a raven and swept off into the night, speeding toward the Pedestrian Mall at the center of the evacuated area.

"Oh, yeah," Hayden said, calming. "I forgot he could turn into a raven."

"Or a wolf," Gabe said. "But I guess a raven was the better choice, this time."

"We can still track him," Hayden said, looking to her phone. "So the tracker works whenever he transforms into something solid, but . . . we're not so lucky when he's smoke."

"Speaking of tracking," Gabe said. "I think that's what

he's doing with the pigeons and cats. Tracking the werewolf. Or maybe just searching for him."

"I agree," Hayden said. "And we'd better follow him, quick. If we lose him again, we can't call him." Gabe nodded at that. Count Drustan, when given his phone, had made it very clear that he'd have no time for any such "toys" during battle.

They ran on.

Hayden was fascinated by the empty streets. It was eerie. But comforting, in a way. Other people always felt like they exuded a sort of pressure, to her. Like she needed to perform. To do . . . *something*. She never knew what. Now, that pressure was gone. She knew she'd miss other people eventually, but for now it was nice to just be Hayden, herself, without feeling everyone else's eyes. She gave a small, private smile as they ran through the streets. They passed a comic book store, the Nine Lives Café, and the sprawling Day Before Day antique emporium. After only a couple of minutes, the Ped Mall was in sight, and none too soon for Hayden, because she was exhausted from running. Luckily, the red dot on her phone had stayed in one place for the last twenty or thirty seconds, giving them a chance to catch up. Maybe the next time she participated in a Versus battle she'd bring a bicycle, or at least a skateboard.

"The pigeons," Gabe said, breathless, as they slowed to a stop at the edges of the Pedestrian Mall, the open mall featuring local stores of all kinds and buildings of all natures. And, as Gabe had noticed, there were pigeons *everywhere*.

They were in the maple and cherry trees. They were perched on windowsills. But mostly they were on the rooftops, lined up and gazing down, hundreds of pigeons eerily lending the Pedestrian Mall the feel of a darkened amphitheater.

"The cats," Hayden said. The cats were harder to notice. They were peeking out from beneath benches. Tucked into recessed doorways. At least fifty cats. Likely more. Cats were good at hiding.

"It's so quiet," Gabe whispered. It felt wrong to disturb the silence.

"I think that's Count Drustan, up there," Hayden whispered back, pointing to the top of the Matador Restaurant, where a large black raven was perched among the pigeons.

"Do you suppose the werewolf is here?" Gabe asked, his eyes wide and alert, clutching his phone in one hand and both of his medallions—his golden vampire medallion and the silver one with the wolf—in his other hand.

"Maybe," Hayden answered. "The pigeons and cats sure seem to think so. It would be strange if the werewolf was *hiding*, though, wouldn't it? Werewolves don't hide, do they?"

"Not really," Gabe said. "But they *do* stalk. If he's here, that's what he's doing. Stalking."

"This is creepy," Hayden whispered. Even as she spoke, another cloud stacked itself in front of the moon, and the darkness grew thicker. Hayden glared up at the clouds.

"I *already* said it was creepy," she complained. Turning her attention back to the Pedestrian Mall, she searched the darkness, walking slowly around a pair of food carts, eyes alert to any movement. She listened to the rising wind. To several awnings fluttering. The hum of distant traffic outside the evacuated area and the chopping *whirrs* of helicopters overhead, seen as nothing more than lights in the dark sky. No werewolves were revealed, but Hayden felt like she could taste danger in the air. She could feel it. The vampire, the raven, took flight across the mall to land on another building, still peering below, with the pigeons again shuffling aside to make room.

"Do you feel it?" Gabe whispered as they edged farther into the mall, walking as if it were a minefield.

"He's here, isn't he?" Hayden said. "The werewolf. He's here." Something inside her knew he was close. Something primal was clenching at her stomach and gripping her heart, sending beads of sweat onto her forehead and making her skin tremble and pucker.

"Yes," Gabe said. "He's here."

CHAPTER 18

Taking a deep, quiet breath in the darkness of the Ped Mall, Hayden tried to remember how she'd reached this point in her life. How had she become a girl who trained vampires for battle with werewolves? Some days she wished she'd remained more . . . normal. She remembered being with her friends Ellie and Mala and Chen at practice four days a week for their school's Iron Petals soccer team, pretending to score winning goals at the World Cup, to the cheering adoration of fans. She remembered the Lucky Bite Ice Cream Shop where they'd all go, having vowed that they would each—one day—devour all sixty-seven of the flavors.

Looking out over the darkened mall, Hayden could almost feel the melt of that ice cream in her mouth. It had seemed, in those days, that the good times would last forever. But then Mala had sat them down one day and told them all about her cancer. In her chest. Gnawing away. The next few months had been heavy with treatment, visiting Mala again and again in the hospital, bringing her ice cream, chatting about life outside the walls of what had virtually become Mala's prison. And all that time it was obvious Mala was slipping away.

One day—visiting Mala in the hospital along with Ellie and Chen—Hayden had tried to feed Mala some ice cream by hand. But Mala was too weak. Too tired. She kept drifting in and out of consciousness. Hayden remembered holding out the ice cream, holding it to Mala's trembling lips and feeling the melting drip of the uneaten ice cream on her wrist. She'd looked to Ellie and Chen, and, though none of them could say it, they understood this might be the last time they saw Mala. Chen ran out in tears, and Ellie hurried off to console her, but Hayden stayed. How could she just . . . *leave*? She'd stayed for an extra hour. And another. It grew dark outside. Hayden nibbled on some snack cookies from her book bag. She hid inside the bathroom whenever a nurse came into the room. Long after visiting hours, Hayden stood watching Mala, flinching at the loudest beeps of the machines, listening for the steps of any nurses in the hall, thinking of Mala's steps whenever she—in those days that seemed long past—sprinted across the soccer field, laughing and joyous, her curled black hair and those little scrunched-nose huffs she'd give whenever she was out of breath, gasping for air, gasping with life. Now, that same girl was gray and motionless. Hayden held Mala's hand and tried to pretend they were still on the soccer field. Still running.

Hayden awoke later in a chair next to the bed, still holding Mala's hand, but knowing something was wrong. At first she thought maybe Mala was . . . gone. Thankfully, there was still a slight rise and fall to her chest. Still the beeping of the monitors. But there was a series of footfalls in the hall outside. Hayden had been hearing nurses for hours. She knew the precise sound of their footfalls.

This was something different.

The footsteps had an extra echo, like they were from a thousand miles away, but also right outside the door. The room grew cold. All the other noises, the general sounds of a hospital at night, were quickly lessening, fading; they were gone. There were only those footsteps coming closer, and then the door opened and Hayden couldn't hide in the bathroom this time. It was too late. Desperate, she slid behind the window curtains, crunching into the corner and trying not to breathe.

Mala's dad walked into the room. But he wasn't alone. Something like a woman was following him, with him coaxing the creature, whispering to it, holding up a glass medallion so that the thing—the *ghost*—could always see it.

And it *was* a ghost. A woman in Victorian clothes. But her skin was decayed. Parts of her were nothing but mist. Moaning low, she exuded a cold that reached Hayden in hiding, behind the curtains. The ghost's footfalls didn't match her footsteps. Hayden cried silent tears. The ghost kept flickering not only in and out of view, but in and out of place as well. One moment she would be in the doorway, then standing next to Mala's bed, and at one point she flickered into sight only inches away from Hayden's hiding spot, so close that Hayden could have reached out and touched the ghost, if such a creature could even be touched at all. The room was covered with frost. The ghostly moans came from everywhere. From the ghost itself. From the walls. The floor. They were filling the room. Filling Hayden's chest.

"This is my daughter," Mala's dad told the ghost, putting his hand on Mala's forehead. The glass medallion, hanging from his other hand on a string of glass beads, clacked in the cold air.

"Your daughter," the ghost said. The words echoed from everywhere. They whispered into Hayden's ears. They scratched at her skin. Hayden wanted to burst out from behind the curtains and run away, run forever.

"Please," Mala's dad said, with such despair in his voice that Hayden nearly choked with emotion. She remembered him as a man who'd cheered during soccer games and who'd donated money so that the team could afford their jerseys. *That* was how she wanted to remember him, not as the sobbing man holding a strange medallion, standing next to his barely living daughter, and a ghost.

"Please," the ghost said. The word filled the room. It felt mocking. The ghostly woman's hands reached out, flickering in more than one place at a time, like several films overlapping, a hundred views of those terrifying hands reaching out. Her hands neared the strange glass medallion but then reached for Mala. The air crackled with cold around her. Mist rose from what served as her flesh. Hayden wanted to explode out from hiding and save Mala from that touch.

But it was too late. The fingers brushed across Mala's chest. And then, with Hayden clamping down on a shriek that nearly gave her away, the ghostly hands slid inside Mala's stomach as if she were made of nothing but air.

"Your daughter," the ghost said, turning to Mala's dad as she—as *it*—pulled her hands free. "Your daughter." The words kept repeating, not as if there was an echo but instead as if the ghost were still speaking the words, though her lips were no longer moving.

"Did you . . . ?" Mala's dad asked. He was shivering, the medallion jerking and swaying as he trembled.

"We are free," the ghost replied. This time her words slashed through the room. The churn of her smoke and mist intensified. Her flesh seemed to breathe, expanding and collapsing, withering and puckering.

"Thank you," Mala's dad said, with a hundred sighs escaping him.

"Your daughter," the ghost said, in not an unkindly fashion. And then she was gone. There was a hissing rush of displaced air filling the void of where she'd been. Hayden kept watch from her hiding spot, terrified the ghost would return, but she didn't. It was only Mala's father, now. He stood by the bed and watched his daughter. He wept so softly that Hayden could barely hear him. He held Mala's hand, and after some time—ten long minutes—he left. Hayden waited for several minutes longer and then stepped out from hiding. She hurried to Mala and touched her cheek, worried her friend would feel cold, like an iceberg, but she was warm. Mala mumbled and slightly stirred. The machines were chirping and beeping. Hayden went to the bathroom—she'd needed to go *so* bad—and sat on the toilet trying to calm her heartbeat, which was still racing, her heart pounding in her chest. In time she managed to leave the hospital and walk home. It was the middle of the night, and her parents were long asleep, thinking she was spending the night at a friend's. She snuck in through the front door and crept slowly up the stairs, careful to avoid the steps that creaked. When she opened the door to her bedroom, the ghost was waiting for her.

The dead woman was floating in the middle of the room, and she swept closer before Hayden could react, bringing her decayed face only an inch away.

"I knew you were there, child," the ghost said. And then she was gone.

Hayden never saw her again.

Over the course of the next two weeks, Mala got better. Day by day, she was stronger. Two months later, she stepped onto the soccer field again, with her joyous tears flung from her cheeks as she raced across the grass, with Hayden and Chen and Ellie running along with her, the soccer ball almost entirely forgotten, the four of them just wanting to run. Mala's cancer had vanished. Like a ghost.

By that time Hayden had learned far more about the world. She'd confronted Mala's father about the ghost. She'd learned about the medallions. And about ghosts. She'd learned about the Versus battles and began searching for medallions of her own. She hadn't entirely left her old life behind and never would, but she'd gained the ability—the knowledge—to step into a new life. She'd learned about witches and mummies and vampires. And . . . werewolves.

"Do you hear that?" Gabe asked.

"No," Hayden said, drawn out from her memories. "Wait. Yes." There was a low rumble in the Pedestrian Mall, coming from inside the Decker Building, the apartment building with the Decker Café on the bottom floor. The building was opposite the side where Count Drustan—still in raven form—was perched. The raven bounded along his perch, first in one direction and then the other. The breeze had transformed into a powerful wind. The maple trees seemed to dance, their branches whipping about. Leaves filled the air. Hayden's tongue felt thick. She clutched her medallions and had the briefest moment of thinking she saw something moving in the darkness behind the Decker Café's front display window, just before the window burst outward in an explosion of glass. A café table had been hurled through with unthinkable force, speeding like a comet across the Ped Mall with a trail of glass behind. The glass clattered on the bricks as the table slammed into the front doors of the Oasis nightclub, crumpling them. Alarms rang out. The wind rose ever stronger, buffeting Hayden and Gabe. A few raindrops began, their numbers quickly growing. The pigeons were having trouble keeping to their perches in the rising storm, but the huge black raven—the vampire—was too strong to be moved.

"He's here," Hayden whispered. "The werewolf is here. Moving through the buildings." The knowledge of the werewolf's presence slid into her stomach, sending acids roiling, her eyes looking up to the third floor of the Decker Building just as the werewolf himself exploded out from an apartment window.

"Oh, *crackers!*" Hayden gasped as the werewolf shattered out through the window on an impossible leap across the mall.

This time it was the werewolf that seemed like a comet, trailing glass behind. He was much bigger than Hayden had expected. Maybe seven feet tall, soaring twenty feet above the ground, his tremendous jump powering him across the Pedestrian Mall, high above the bricks below. The heavy wind ripped at his fur. The glass fell to the ground, but the werewolf continued onward, having aimed himself at the vampire across the void. The beast sped through the wind and the rain, the moon lighting him from behind, his terrible claws reaching out for the raven. The vampire fluttered backward in a sudden panic, his wings flapping in furious fashion as the werewolf came closer and closer, the gap narrowing, the creature's roar so loud, the flock of pigeons scattering, the glass falling all around. The werewolf's claws slashed through the air and sent black feathers out in a puff, with the raven knocked backward as the werewolf tumbled out of sight atop the roof so far above. Hayden strained to see what was happening, but the angles were wrong. She and Gabe were on the ground, but her vampire—and the werewolf—were on the rooftops.

"We have to get up there!" Hayden shouted, looking hurriedly around. How could they possibly reach the rooftops? All the doors would be locked. Was there a fire escape they could use?

"There!" Gabe shouted, pointing at the Oasis nightclub and the broken doors.

"Good thinking!" Hayden yelled as the rain began pouring violently down from the sky, with dark clouds rumbling, drowning out even the alarms. Hayden and Gabe, already soaking wet, began moving the table from the doorway, but before they could finish, an outraged howl blared from the rooftops above, and then the werewolf came arcing down over the edge, spinning out of control, slamming into a maple tree and then colliding with one of the solidly built benches at the edges of a flower bed, cracking bricks with the power of his impact. For a moment the beast seemed stunned, and that was enough time for Gabe and Hayden—only ten yards away—to bring up their silver medallions, holding them out for protection as the huge creature shook his head in pain, the rainwater flung from his fur, his fangs glistening in the moonlight; then he sprang unthinkably quick to his feet and charged forward, scrambling on all fours, claws scratching deep lines into the bricks, only pulling up short when his eyes went wide at the sight of the medallions. The werewolf's fangs snapped at the air as he tried to quickly circle behind Gabe and Hayden, but they turned with him, keeping their medallions between themselves and the terrifying beast. It howled in frustration, a bestial sound, utterly inhuman, but then just as quickly laughed in a manner so bizarrely human that it made Gabe gasp, and his grip on his medallion loosened, but it didn't matter. The werewolf had forgotten him. It sprang up and over Gabe and Hayden into the side of the building, where his claws bit deep as he began to clamber upward. But he'd only managed a few feet before the vampire came over the roof's edge in a terrifying form that was half man, half bat, soaring downward to rip the werewolf off the building, hurling him once more to the ground.

The eerily half-human vampire bat swooped to a stop on the Ped Mall, transforming fully back to his true form to stand on the bricks, faced off against the werewolf, which was snarling in rage as it regained its feet. Count Drustan was in his three-piece tweed check suit, with the wind and rain barely seeming to touch him, as if he was immune to nature itself.

"I hope you're ready for this," the vampire told the werewolf.

CHAPTER 19

Joon and Tradd hurried through the rising storm, following the cats to the Pedestrian Mall ahead. The heavy rain had come from nowhere. The wind buffeted Joon so fiercely that she felt unsteady on her feet. She and Tradd ran down the middle of the street. It felt strange. All her life she knew better than to run in the street, but this section of Tacoma was deserted, now. There was only herself. Only Tradd. Only the cats running ahead of them, oddly enduring a rain that would normally send them scurrying for cover.

The darkness was resolute. Closing in around them. The dark clouds were blocking the moonlight. Joon knew the darkness wouldn't hinder the monsters, though. They could see in the night. Better than any human. Better than any animal. They were otherworldly creatures. The darkness wouldn't stop them. The oncoming storm wouldn't stop them. The werewolf could only be stopped by the vampire, and the vampire only by the werewolf. Who would win? Joon dashed deeper into the storm and the darkness, needing to know.

Tradd's glasses fogged up. His shoes were soaked from splashing through the growing puddles. There was no time to bother with any of it.

"We're missing the battle!" Joon yelled. "Can you hear them?" The howls from ahead were as loud as the storm.

"I can't *not* hear them!" Tradd replied.

"I'm super scared to meet a vampire!" Joon yelled as they ran. A few sharp pellets of hail slammed down around them, a few others actually into them. The cats had disappeared into the darkness ahead. The hailstones clacked against the asphalt, the concrete, the brick buildings, and the windows. The wind howled. The werewolf in the distance howled, too. Tradd grabbed Joon's hand, warm in the night, and together they ran through the heavy storm, through the rain and hail, along an entirely deserted street in a time of darkness, to the battle between a vampire and a werewolf.

With Tradd at her side, Joon hurried into the Ped Mall. Her feet crunched across what she first thought was hail on the bricks, but quickly realized was glass from broken windows. Thunder rumbled through her bones as lightning crashed through the skies above, illuminating the scene. Some forty feet away, Hayden and Gabe were huddled beneath an awning in front of the Oasis nightclub. And in the middle of the mall, Redd Sampayo—the werewolf—had his back against a maple tree, and his jaws locked around a vampire's arm.

"They're really here," Joon said in a voice soft with awe, heard only because a deafening roar of thunder had just faded. The driving rain was a constant backdrop, a million drumbeats of impact on the bricks and buildings. The vampire was smaller than Joon had expected. But of course that was only because he was standing next to a seven-foot-tall werewolf, or rather, *not* standing but being hurled away, cast off like a broken chew toy.

"Oh," Tradd grunted. The vampire—flung aside—was hurtling toward the front windows of the Speedy Sports Bar. It seemed impact was inevitable, but suddenly the vampire changed into an enormous bat and swerved aside, landing on the bricks and then changing into an even more enormous wolf, which howled and snarled.

"Wolf against werewolf," Joon breathed out, shielding her face against the storm. "C'mon!" She took Tradd's hand again. "Let's watch with Hayden and Gabe! Under that awning!" Together, they began hurrying toward the others, but their movement gained the wolf's attention. It sprang in front of them, as big as a horse, the jaws easily large enough to snap them up. Joon was knocked backward, flailing and stumbling to the bricks. A paw pinned her down. Then the paw became a hand, and she was staring up into the vampire's face.

He was a handsome man. Dark eyes. Stonelike cheekbones. A slightly arched nose. The rainwater coursed through his dark hair, down over his face to drip from his fangs. His hand felt harder than the bricks beneath her. It felt colder.

He was a vampire and he was hungry.

"Precious blood," he said, looking to Joon like a meal. "Some warmth for me in this sweet dark night." His fangs dropped closer. Joon struggled beneath him, but his hunger was far beyond her strength, and she felt the cold sting of his fangs on her throat.

Two things happened, then.

The first was that Tradd knelt suddenly beside Joon and literally thrust a medallion against the vampire's forehead, ordering him, "Back! *Back!* Stay back from her!"

And the second thing that happened meant that the first thing didn't matter, because before the vampire could react to Tradd and the medallion, the werewolf slammed into him from the side. The tremendous impact sent them both tumbling, ripping the vampire away from Joon. The two creatures smashed into a wooden bench and reduced it to kindling, then crashed into the thick concrete bricks of a raised planter bed, which cracked but held, sending the two monsters bouncing upward to slam into the trunk of a maple tree. The werewolf's claws raked across the vampire's chest. Count Drustan bit deep into the werewolf's shoulder. Redd kicked outward and gouged along the vampire's side. The vampire threw a punch that barely missed the werewolf's jaw. The werewolf grabbed Count Drustan with both hands and slammed him to the ground with an impact that rumbled as loudly as the thunder above. The vampire was stunned. Weak with pain. Helpless.

Howling in triumph, the werewolf stood above the stricken vampire. His roar was entirely bestial. There seemed to be nothing human left. Joon shivered to think how close the vampire's fangs had come to sinking into her neck, and was equally chilled by how the werewolf—a creature that had stalked her in the forested warehouse—could triumph against such a force.

The werewolf struck, slashing a clawed hand down at the fallen vampire, but the werewolf's howls of triumph had come too soon and taken too long, giving Count Drustan a chance to recover. Before the werewolf's claws struck, the vampire transformed to smoke, the beast's claws slashing through nothing. The smoke billowed upward, wrapping around the werewolf, covering his face. It slid into his nose and mouth. Panic lit the beast's eyes as he fought against nothing, his claws futilely slashing the air all around as he staggered across the bricks. The hail pummeled everything, ripping through the maple trees and sending tattered leaves falling amid the heavy rain. To Tradd, watching the battle, each hailstone felt like a punch. He needed cover. He needed—

A hand came down on his shoulder. He nearly screamed.

But it was just Gabe, pulling him back, with Hayden helping Joon to her feet. "Get under the awning!" Gabe yelled in order to be heard over the thunder, the hail, the rain, and the werewolf's outraged howls.

"Thanks!" Tradd told Gabe, staggering with the others across the small gulf to reach shelter, though it was a precarious shelter at best. The wind was trying to rip the awning free, with powerful gusts slashing the rain almost sideways through the air. Tradd had to hope that the helicopters could remain in the air, despite the storm. If not, the Wardens and the Crafters couldn't stay close. Tradd looked to the skies, peering into the darkness to see if any helicopter lights were still visible. They weren't.

"Looking for helicopters?" Gabe asked, yelling above the chaos. "I think they're gone. I tried to call Meeda, but the call wouldn't go through."

"I think we're alone," Hayden told Tradd. "With them." She pointed to the monsters just as three strokes of lightning crashed through the skies above, one after the other. The thunder rumbled the ground as the terrible wind and hail tore at the trees and the awnings, the weather so brutal that Tradd was forced to shield his eyes as he watched the battle unfold between the werewolf and the vampire.

The werewolf had no means to fight the smoke. It was in his eyes. His mouth. His lungs. He was being battered from within, fighting an opponent who was effectively intangible. The werewolf kept slashing at the air, but his claws found nothing to shred. His fangs kept gnashing at the smoke, but the smoke could not be bitten. The werewolf was a simple creature. He had no other weapons besides claws, fangs, and muscle, and none of them were proving to be of any worth against the odd smoke that was assaulting him, the smoke that was—in truth—a vampire, dead for hundreds of years, but still walking the earth, and winning the fight.

The werewolf roared. He howled. Louder and louder until he seemed to be pushing back the storm.

"He's frustrated," Hayden said. She smiled. Her vampire was winning the battle.

"He's smart," Joon corrected Hayden, and Hayden looked to her, wondering what she meant. Smart? The werewolf was doing nothing but, in effect, screaming. How was *that* smart?

But Joon understood that the werewolf, while bestial past all comprehension, was still a man. He wasn't—entirely—a creature of rage. He was a man who'd built a forest in a warehouse. A man who'd nurtured an ecosystem. Beneath all that fur and rage, behind all those claws and teeth, was a man of science. A man who understood that *everything* could be touched. Even smoke. And where his fangs and claws failed, sound waves could succeed.

With each roar, the vampiric smoke shuddered. With each howl, the smoke flinched. Joon could remember being too close to speakers at concerts, the way they felt like they were literally slamming the music against her. And the deafening roar of the thunder in the skies was more than just a sound: it was a physical presence, a wave of force that shoved everything aside. That was what the werewolf was doing, battering the vampiric smoke with sound. The smoke jerked with each roar. Swirled with each howl. And, finally, the smoke drew back and transformed once more into the vampire, Count Drustan, who staggered away from the werewolf, clutching his chest, one leg nearly limp, dragging behind as he desperately tried to gain some distance between himself and the seven-foot-tall engine of destruction that was the werewolf.

"Too slow," Joon said. And she was right. A vampire recovers quickly, but nothing recovers faster than a werewolf. Wounds heal in seconds. Exhaustion is all but unknown. A werewolf is relentless. The rain washed over him, the wind battered him, the golf-ball-size hail slammed into him from the skies, and none of it mattered to the creature. It only added to his joy. There is nothing a werewolf loves more than chaos, and there is nothing that chaos loves more than a werewolf.

CHAPTER 20

The werewolf sprang to the attack. It was a leap that covered twenty feet. Count Drustan managed to snatch the beast out of midair, grabbing him by the throat, but it was a mistake. Never grapple with a werewolf. The beast sank his jaws into the vampire's shoulder even as his hand circled the vampire's throat, squeezing with literally monstrous strength. The vampire punched the werewolf in reply, a fist that shattered bone, but the werewolf did not release his hold. His broken jaw healed in moments. The moon was shining bright. The awning above the onlookers—Joon and Tradd and Hayden and Gabe—flapped like an enormous wing, the metal struts shrieking in outrage. The wind and hail ripped the maple trees to shreds, their tattered leaves swirling between the buildings, caught in the storm.

"It's so *cold*!" Gabe yelled to Hayden. The hail clattered to the bricks all around, shattering with impact, spraying them with ice.

"We need better shelter!" Tradd said. "Somewhere inside!"

"All the doors will be locked!" Joon said.

"Maybe over there?" he answered, pointing across the Ped Mall to the shattered front window of the Decker Café, where the werewolf had hurled a table through the glass.

"Can we make it?" Hayden asked. They all knew what she meant. Despite the terrible wind, rain, and hail, they could stagger their way to safety, but there was an even bigger problem than the storm unleashing its fury on the city below: the monsters.

"We *can't* stay here!" Joon yelled, forced to scream in order to be heard by the others, even though they were huddled closely together. And then, as if in emphasis to her words, the awning began tearing free from its moorings. A tremendous gust ripped it upward, tearing it partially free from the wall. Another gust slammed it downward like a giant hand, slapping both Hayden and Tradd to the bricks. The awning was like a frenzied animal struggling for freedom against a leash, bucking and tugging at the wall, the wind howling all around.

Gabe helped the dazed Hayden to her feet and partially supported her as they hurried away from what seemed to be an enraged awning. Forty feet away, the werewolf was choking the vampire, with furred hands around a throat that was already cold and dead, but living still, at least for now, unless the werewolf had his way. The struggle had them rolling across the bricks, tossed here and there by the force of their brawl, much like the helpless maple leaves swirling all over the Ped Mall, caught in the fierce wind.

"Don't get too close to them!" Hayden mumbled, blinking.

"No way," Gabe agreed, looking to the battle. The vampire was losing. He couldn't break the werewolf's grip from around his throat. In a battle of strength, Count Drustan would actually win, even against a werewolf. But this wasn't only a battle of pure muscle; it was also one of ferocity, and the sheer brutality of the werewolf wasn't allowing the vampire to gain his balance.

"This hurts!" Tradd gasped, caught in the open hailstorm with the others as they hurried across the Ped Mall, hoping to gain shelter inside the Decker Café. He had one arm up to protect his head, and his other arm helping to shield Joon. The hail felt like fists. The rain drove at him, and the wind kept blowing leaves and garbage across his face, with the stronger gusts making him feel disturbingly light on his feet, as if the wind was attempting to snatch him into the air, up into the heart of the storm.

There was no way the helicopters were still in the skies. The Wardens, the Crafters, the doctors, they'd undoubtedly all been grounded, pushed to the sidelines. Tradd knew the four of them were alone with the monsters, now.

Isolated. Cut off from all others. The Wardens couldn't even move through the streets. The storm was too dangerous. Even this short dash across the mall was a risk.

Together, the four Trainers did their best to hurry across the open area, huddling together for protection. Even though it was no more than eighty feet away, the Decker Café kept fading from view, lost not only in the darkness and the rain but also a thickly gathering fog, rising from the bricks. Gabe peered through the mist while listening to the roars of the werewolf in the fog. How was the battle going? The last Gabe had seen, it looked bad for Count Drustan, with those powerful werewolf hands around his throat. Gabe could hear the sounds of impact, of struggle, but everything else was lost in the storm. They hadn't at all planned for the storm. The weather report hadn't mentioned any possibility. Gabe had thought he'd be watching the battle from a safe distance, away from the werewolf and the vampire, and away from Tradd and Joon, but now this terrible storm—a storm that had seemed to leap out from hiding—had drawn them all together. It had *pushed* them together.

"Hurry!" Joon encouraged the others, impatient as a herd dog. Gabe heard a sharp cracking noise and looked up to see a huge tree branch give way, a victim of the heavy wind. Shifting his grip on Hayden, he quickly reached out to yank Joon backward, the three of them falling to the ground as the branch crashed to the bricks where Joon had been standing.

"Oh, *lemons*," she breathed out. "Thanks!" The branch

had only grazed her legs, the impact minimal. The wind was already tumbling the branch away, nudging it along the bricks. A werewolf's howl of outrage and pain broke through the mist and fog. There came the sound of heavy impact from somewhere in the darkness. Tradd had a sense of something in the air. Hayden was having trouble focusing. Everything was a blur. Struggling to his feet, Gabe felt his senses flare, a warning burst of electricity through his veins, a wave of panic as his mind and body registered that something was *wrong*, and then he was brutally struck from behind. Flung back to the bricks. It felt as if he'd been hit by a car. A building. A mountain.

But it was the werewolf.

Together, Gabe and the werewolf sprawled on the bricks. Side by side. Inches apart. Gabe ached from the impact. Had the werewolf attacked him? It didn't seem that way. Instead, the beast had been . . . hurled from afar? Cast from the battle? And now the monster was only inches away. Gabe's hand weakly clutched at . . . nothing? Where were his medallions? They'd been knocked free. Frantically searching through the hailstones and leaves, Gabe's fingers wrapped around the chain of his golden vampire medallion. Then he saw the glinting silver of his werewolf medallion only a couple of feet away, but before he could convince his muscles to move, a fist-size chunk of hail knocked the medallion farther away, sending it tumbling and dancing across the bricks, sliding beneath the branch that had fallen from the maple tree.

"Peanuts," Gabe cursed, feeling the cold night grow even colder.

"Foolish," he heard. A voice he didn't recognize. It wasn't Hayden or Joon or Tradd, and it definitely wasn't Count Drustan. It was a rougher voice. Scratching and brutal. The werewolf was speaking to him.

"Foolish," the werewolf repeated. Gabe slowly turned from his lost medallion and, afraid of what he would see, looked to the werewolf.

The beast was struggling to rise. Grievous wounds healed in front of Gabe's eyes. Torn fur rippled back into place. The werewolf leaned on one arm, rolling closer to Gabe so that his jaws were only inches above Gabe. The head was so large that it almost counted as shelter, protecting Gabe from the storm. The werewolf barely seemed to notice him at first, but then the strange eyes—gray with red at the edges—tilted downward. Then came a rumbling growl that Gabe could feel.

"Foolish," the werewolf repeated.

"Foolish?" Gabe asked, immediately feeling like he'd answered his own question. The foolish thing was . . . to talk with the werewolf. The creature could kill him with minimal effort. Why invite any attention? It was best to stay quiet and hope he was simply beneath the beast's notice, since he was literally beneath his jaws.

"Me," the werewolf rasped out. "I'm foolish."

"Foolish?" Gabe asked again, which was, again, foolish.

"Trying to choke a vampire," the werewolf said, with something like a sigh. The smell of his sodden fur was like mold. His breath was visible in the cool air. He closed his eyes for long moments and then opened them, staring at Gabe, running a claw across Gabe's stomach.

"What do vampires need, child?" he asked. His words were grating. Bestial. Gabe didn't know what to say. He clamped his mouth tight. Words felt wrong. Everything felt wrong.

"I asked what vampires need, boy," the werewolf said. The claw pressed onto Gabe's stomach, not quite cutting.

"Blood?" Gabe answered, stuttering the word, both from the chill in the air and the chill in his gut.

"Blood," the werewolf agreed. "The answer is simple. It's the *only* answer. It's a vampire's single and solitary need. And yet, I tried to choke the *breath* from him. Foolish. Vampires don't need air. They need blood." Putting a huge hand on Gabe's chest, the werewolf pressed down, but only so that he could stand. Soon, the creature's entire seven feet towered above Gabe. The beast took one long stride, stepping to the massive branch that had fallen from the tree, easily picking it up with one hand before tossing it aside. Reaching down, the werewolf picked up the silver medallion, its power lessened since Gabe wasn't holding it. The werewolf studied it closely for one heartbeat, the wind blowing fiercely at his fur, hailstones bouncing off his muscled flesh, seemingly unnoticed. He sniffed at the medallion, and his nose scrunched in disgust. With a casual gesture, he tossed the medallion to Gabe. It bounced off his chest.

"Do not lose that again," the werewolf snarled. "Or I could kill you." The beast turned, then, and hurried off to rejoin his battle with the vampire.

CHAPTER 21

Grabbing his medallion, Gabe watched the werewolf loping away on all fours, the beast howling in delight as the moon momentarily emerged from the dark clouds above. Then the clouds closed again and the darkness held sway. The sudden fog rolled away, blown by the fierce wind. A cat meowed in panic from somewhere. Alarms still rang out from all around. But as Gabe stood, a sense of calm slid over him. He'd survived.

"Gabe!" he heard. It was Hayden. She frantically patted him down, looking for any injuries. "Oh, my gosh and crackers! Are you okay? Did he—?"

"I'm fine!" Gabe assured her. "I mean, I'm kinda overdosed on terror, but the werewolf was . . . he didn't hurt me. And never mind *that*, we have to get out of this hail!" The hailstones were growing larger. Most of the incoming missiles were still no bigger than a golf ball, but a few were baseball-size. Staying outside was too dangerous. All around, the puddles were growing into streams, rivers, and lakes. The water had a current, and the hail kept pounding down from above, driving into the water with hollow *thoom*-ing noises.

"Let's go!" Joon urged, hurrying up to Gabe and Hayden. Tradd was with her, bleeding from his cheek. He noticed Gabe looking to the blood.

"Got hit by a . . . ," he began explaining, but before he could finish, a massive chunk of hail slammed into the side of his head with a slushing *clap* of impact, and Tradd's knees buckled. Gabe grabbed him before he could fall, holding him upright while looking into Tradd's eyes, which were clearly unfocused, barely conscious.

"Is he okay?" Joon yelled in fright.

"Let's go!" Gabe shouted, picking up Tradd as best as he could, slinging him over his shoulder and staggering off toward the broken café window. They *needed* to reach cover. Gabe felt terrible about how Tradd was acting as his unfortunate shield against the incoming hail. He heard a couple of more sudden thumps and a matching set of groans from Tradd, and then they were finally at the window and Gabe was carefully stepping through, mindful that neither he nor Tradd came into contact with the broken glass still caught in the picture window's frame.

"Over here!" Joon said, standing inside, backlit by the café's emergency lights, gesturing for Gabe to hurry. She swept a table free of a napkin dispenser and then stood back as Gabe put Tradd down on the table, with Tradd's legs hanging off the edge.

"M'okay," Tradd muttered, trying to sit up. Joon pushed him back down and adjusted his glasses into place.

"Don't move," she ordered. "The sky got very angry and clobbered you. How many fingers am I holding up?" She held three fingers in front of his face.

He looked in the wrong direction and said, "Heck, yeah. Cake."

"Oh, dang," she whispered.

"Right," Hayden said. "He *definitely* needs a few minutes. But first things first; does everyone have both of their medallions?"

"I do," Gabe said, holding up his vampire medallion and the lesser werewolf medallion.

"I've got both of mine," Joon said, "but I can't find Tradd's vampire medallion." She was checking his pockets, making sure it wasn't tucked into his shirt or anywhere else. "It's gone."

"He must have lost it in the storm," Hayden said. "We'll have to make do with the medallions we have. As long as we stay in good cover, we can last until Count Drustan wins, and then we'll get Tradd to a doctor."

"After *Redd* wins, you mean," Joon said.

"Redd?" Gabe asked. "Who's that?"

"Redd Sampayo. The werewolf. He's going to win."

"A werewolf can't win against a vampire," Gabe said. "That's ridiculous. You don't understand how powerful Count Drustan is."

"*You* don't understand werewolves," Joon replied, her voice growing angry. She hurried off to the café's refrigerator to get some ice, wrapped it in a towel, and pressed it to Tradd's head. He tried to wave her away, but his eyes were unfocused and his efforts were weak.

"I understand enough about werewolves to know that Count Drustan has been playing with him," Hayden said.

"Playing?" Joon asked in disbelief. "Is that what you call getting slashed open?"

"Your werewolf got tossed from a roof. Choked with smoke."

"Choked with smoke *until* Redd roared, you mean. For all the supposed power of your vampire, Redd only had to howl and Drustan was nearly beaten right there."

"Our vampire has been gaining in power for hundreds of years," Gabe hissed, his fingers clenching. Joon couldn't possibly believe a werewolf could beat a vampire, could she? He paced about. The storm outside was investigating the broken window, with strong winds bursting inside, blowing menus to the floor. The hail bounced against the broken window's edges, knocking remnants of glass from the frame. Puddles formed even on the café floor.

"Well, I'm *so* glad Drustan's been growing more powerful for hundreds of years," Joon mocked. "Maybe he should've napped for a couple hundred *more* years, though, because he's getting his butt kicked tonight." She held up her secondary vampire medallion, then stared Gabe in the eyes and dropped it to the floor, adding, "Whoops! One vampire down."

"You shouldn't lose that," Gabe said, pointing to the medallion.

"Oh, yeah," Joon said, somewhat embarrassed, picking it up. "I got a little carried away." Holding her medallions, she moved away from Tradd after giving his hand a comforting squeeze. He squeezed back, which was a good sign, but they needed to get him to a doctor. Unfortunately, the fight outside needed to end before that could possibly happen. In a normal Versus battle, there were doctors at hand in case someone got injured, but today the doctors had been in the helicopters, and because of the unexpected storm, the helicopters were gone. Now, Joon and the others were trapped in the storm, isolated until the monsters finished their fight.

"I'm going out there," she said. "Just to look. I need to know what's happening." She was standing near the shattered picture window, gazing out into the storm. There was no sign of the vampire or the werewolf. Joon brought up the tracking device on her phone, but the monsters weren't registering.

"I can't find them on the tracker," she said. "Maybe because of the storm?"

"Maybe," Hayden said, looking to her own phone. "I'm not getting any locations, either. Not even us. If we don't know where the monsters are at, it's too risky to go out. Let's face it, both of our monsters have entirely forgotten the rule about not killing each other. They've gone primal. Far too dangerous to be around. And that storm outside is terrible."

"But I need to know," Joon said, swallowing, looking out to the storm. "If . . . if Redd loses the fight, I lose my medallion. I mean, he *won't* lose the fight, but if he *does*—ah, *lemons*! I don't even want to think about it! I can't just . . . stand here! I'm going out."

"You can't go out alone," Hayden argued. "And we can't leave Tradd. He's only half-conscious and doesn't have one of his medallions."

"I'll stay with him," Gabe offered. "I took the Wardens' First Aid Training Course. I'll do what I can to help him. The two of you find his medallion so we can all leave."

"Sounds like a plan," Joon said. Hayden was more reluctant. Leave her partner? Go out into the storm? That didn't seem smart. But nothing seemed smart, and they had to do something.

"Let's use these serving trays for cover," Hayden said, picking up a pair of large plastic serving trays and handing one to Joon.

"Thanks," Joon said, holding the tray over her head as she stepped back out into the storm. The wind tried to rip the tray from Joon's hands, making her stagger about, with the tray acting almost as a sail, but the constant crash of hailstones atop the tray made her think twice about leaving it behind. With Hayden following, she hurried to where Tradd had been injured. His vampire medallion *had* to be somewhere.

"See it?" Hayden asked, searching all over the bricks, brushing leaves aside.

"No," Joon replied. There were so many places the medallion could be hiding. Under the leaves, or possibly even underwater, because the puddles were huge now. What if it was lost? What would they do? She knelt in the cold puddles, frantically sloshing her hand through the chilling water with the floating hailstones.

"C'mon, c'mon!" she muttered. Her hand was cold. This would be so simple if she had magic. Someday, if she made it through this night and this fight between monsters, she could become a witch and find medallions with ease. Maybe she could even *make* medallions. But she needed to win tonight. She needed the werewolf to beat the vampire.

"I hear them," Hayden said, standing suddenly.

"Where?" Joon asked. "What did you hear?" But then, a strange gust of air rushed past her? No, it was more than the wind. It had physical presence. A monstrosity.

"What was—?" she started to ask, but then she saw a shape slash through the sky, flying in front of the clouds. A man? A flicker of lightning illuminated the skies so that for one brief moment Joon could see the man better, and then he dive-bombed toward the bricks of the Ped Mall, riding the violent air currents with ease. He pulled up at the last second and came to a running landing. It was the vampire. Count Drustan.

He was half man. Half bat. A terrifying bat head on a man's body, with wings to his sides. He let out a screech that felt like daggers in Joon's ears. There was a rush of movement as the werewolf sprang out of a doorway, leaping for the vampire, but Count Drustan spread his wings and let the storm winds take him, instantly swept back up into the air, avoiding the werewolf's charge. Redd changed his attack, however, using a bench as a launching pad to leap high in the air and slash at the vampire. But Count Drustan was ready for that as well, and—with a simple flap of his wings that whisked him beyond the werewolf's reach—he then used the brutal air currents to speed after the werewolf as the beast was helplessly falling, the power of his leap exhausted. The vampire clamped on to the beast's shoulder with the bat-like claws of his feet. A few flaps of his wings and the vampire carried the werewolf higher. Thirty feet. Forty. Fifty and sixty and a hundred. He went ever higher into the darkened sky, deeper into the terrible storm, battered from all sides but still climbing into the night. Redd struggled, but the vampire kept his grip secure, and there was nothing the werewolf could do.

"He's going to drop him," Joon whispered, watching the ascent with horror. She felt a clutch in her chest. Redd was . . . terrifying. But she'd gotten to know him, and he wasn't always a terror. Sometimes he was kind. Sometimes he was the man who'd built January Memorial Forest in memory of his mother. And now he was high above the bricks, caught in a storm, caught in a vampire's grip, and about to be dropped.

"He won't drop him," Hayden said with certainty. Joon looked to her in relief, but then Hayden added, "If I know the vampire, he's going to *throw* him." And she was right. Even as she spoke, with the monsters nearly three hundred feet above, the vampire flew in a tight loop, using the added force to hurl the werewolf down toward the waiting bricks. Just as Count Drustan released the werewolf, a flash of lightning illuminated the scene. In the bright light, Hayden and Joon could see the werewolf's frantically flailing limbs waving through the air, desperately reaching back for the vampire, but it was already too late. There was nothing to save him. His roar of outrage shook the skies as loud as the thunder. He was falling, and there was nothing to be done. He fell for twenty feet. Thirty. Fifty. And then another flash of lightning, but this time the lightning did more than illuminate the scene. The bolt struck the werewolf, momentarily making him as bright as the sun. The lightning swatted the werewolf from the skies as if he'd been struck by an enormous godlike hammer. Redd fell limp, battered by the hail, falling with the rain, amid the vampire's mocking laughter.

The werewolf crashed into the side of the Paramount Building, right next to Gentlemen's Best Clothiers, where

Count Drustan had purchased his suit. He rebounded off the building to slam to the bricks of the Ped Mall, splashing into a puddle, bouncing once and then twice, helpless and unconscious, still with flickers of electricity flowing over his smoldering fur, his limbs limp and his jaws agape. The creature rolled to a stop no more than twenty feet away, face down in another of the deep flowing puddles.

"Redd!" Joon yelled. She ran to the werewolf's side and did her best to simultaneously hold the serving tray above her head while holding the werewolf's head out of the water so he wouldn't drown. But it was all too much. The werewolf was too heavy, especially when she was struggling with one hand, but it was too risky to put down the tray and take her chances with the hailstones. She was slipping into panic, lost in the chaos of the battle and the storm, the hail slamming into the tray above her head, crashing into the bricks and plunging into the waters, striking powerful blows on the werewolf, with the security alarms from all around seeming to burn into her brain.

"Hayden!" Joon yelled. "I need help!" Patches of the werewolf's fur had been fused together or burned away. His eyes kept fluttering open. Fluttering closed. His fingers twitched. Every time Joon thought she'd finally raised his head completely free of the water, his enormous body would twist as he fought to regain consciousness, and then his head would slip back under the surface. Finally, Joon simply discarded the tray, trusting herself to fate, although fate hadn't been very kind, so far.

With both hands free, she was able to move the werewolf better. She flipped him completely over onto his back and got her knees under his head for support, lifting him from the water. He moaned and said something unintelligible, his eyes only slits. The hailstones kept crashing all around. The noise was thunderous. Joon could barely think. But she had to help Redd. She had to risk the hail. The waters all around her were splashing with impact, and then a hailstone hit her arm. She dropped the werewolf, her arm stunned, and he sank back under the water. Cursing, Joon hefted him back to the surface, again holding him against her knees. And then a hailstone struck her head. It felt like being hit by a club. She saw white. A flash of yellows and purples. Blood burst from her forehead, the warmth of it strange in the cold rain. She felt her limbs go slack. Redd slipped under the water again. Joon fought to stay conscious and to lift the werewolf from beneath the water. Water ran through his wet fur, and he said something again, mumbling despite not being conscious. Joon was trying to decide what the werewolf was saying when it suddenly occurred to her that—despite having tossed her tray aside—she was again hearing the distinctive clacking of the hail hitting the plastic tray over her head. Looking up, she found Hayden standing above her, protecting them both with her own tray, occasionally yelping whenever the hail struck her fingers.

"Thanks!" Joon yelled, cradling the werewolf's head.

"It was the least I could do," Hayden said. "Because—"

But whatever she was going to say next was lost, because the vampire came from the skies above, landing only a few feet away, once more fully a man. He straightened his ruined clothes. He glanced at the werewolf and then focused entirely on Joon. On her forehead. His eyes went red, and his lips pulled back to reveal his fangs.

"Your forehead, girl," he said, staring into her eyes. "You're *bleeding*."

"Oh no," Joon whispered.

CHAPTER 22

Gabe had done everything possible for Tradd, using not only the knowledge he'd gained from his first aid training with the Wardens, but also the summer he'd spent helping the medical trainer for his dad's college baseball team. He'd bound Tradd's head with bandages found in a first aid kit. Gotten him some ice. If it looked like Tradd might fall asleep, Gabe kept him awake, because sleeping could be dangerous for people with concussions, and Tradd certainly had one.

He'd tried to call Meeda or Quinn Obermark, or anyone. None of the calls went through. The storm was too intense. He even tried to call Hayden. No luck. The trackers still weren't working, either. His phone was almost useless.

"If I was a warlock . . . ," he mumbled, letting the words dwindle away, although his thoughts did not.

Tradd mumbled. Gabe looked to him. Maybe he couldn't help Tradd with magic, but he could definitely help in other ways.

"I'll try to find you a pillow," Gabe told Tradd, and listened to him mutter something in reply. Gabe had already pulled another table next to the one where Tradd was sprawled, merging the two together so that Tradd's legs weren't hanging off the edge anymore.

"These will do," Gabe told himself, grabbing a stack of towels and clumping them together into a makeshift pillow. He nabbed a couple of muffins from a display case, ate one, and offered the other to Tradd, who frowned at the blueberry muffin as if it were an alien creature, so Gabe ate that one too, even though he wasn't actually hungry. Just nervous. The rain and the hail and the vampire and the werewolf, they were all outside. And *Hayden* was there, too. What if she was in trouble when all *he* was doing was sitting in a chair next to Tradd, munching on two muffins?

"It was wrong to let her go out there," he mumbled to himself. He thought of the vampire outside. The werewolf. Even Joon. Could she be trusted? She was on the other team. And the weather was arguably the most dangerous of all. Tradd could attest to that.

"How are you feeling?" he asked Tradd.

"A little better," Tradd said. His voice was shaky. But it was the first time he'd actually answered a question instead of just babbling. "I think I was . . ." His voice trailed off.

"What?" Gabe asked.

"Dreaming. I heard a dog bark. Keeper. My dog. He's a terrier. Missing." Tradd's words were hesitant. Whispery. Chopped. He clutched at his werewolf medallion.

"You really took a knock," Gabe said, looking in Tradd's eyes, making sure they were focused behind those round red glasses.

"What happened?"

"A big ol' hailstone smacked you in your skull."

"That's why it hurts?" Tradd asked, rubbing the side of his head. He tried to sit up, but couldn't find the strength.

"That's why it hurts," Gabe said, putting a hand on Tradd's chest, pushing down, making sure Tradd didn't stand until he was ready.

"Is the fight over?" Tradd asked, settling back down on the table.

"Don't know. Haven't seen the monsters for a while." He hoped Count Drustan was okay. The battle was fiercer than Gabe had expected. The werewolf was brutal and terrifying, and while it was true that the vampire was a horrifying creature who lived on blood, he was also a man who'd strolled through this very area only a few days ago, giving Hayden a soft smile after helping identify the sphinx medallions, and—in a moment Gabe still thought was funny, even though he was aware that maybe he *shouldn't* think it was funny—Count Drustan had set those pigeons on the terrible guitar player. Gabe wondered if maybe some of those same pigeons were the ones outside, now, in the storm. He hoped the birds were okay. He hoped the vampire was okay, too.

"Where's Joon?" Tradd's hand waved in the air, as if trying to find her.

"Outside. With Hayden. They're trying to find your vampire medallion."

"It fell," Tradd said. "I think I'm going to sleep, now. I can't stay awake."

"Well, that's a problem, because I'm not letting you sleep. I'll pour ice water up your nose."

"Annoying," Tradd said. "Thanks, though. I suppose I shouldn't sleep. Concussion. Right?"

"That's how it is," Gabe said.

"I'm hungry. Do concussions make you hungry?"

"I don't think so? I offered you a blueberry muffin, but you didn't want it."

"Really? What was I thinking? Are there more?"

"Yeah. Hold on." Gabe gave Tradd a pat on the shoulder and walked around the back of the counter to grab a muffin. There were only strawberry muffins left, but Tradd was just going to have to live with it.

"Muffin," Gabe announced, walking back out from around the counter, looking up to Tradd and . . . a girl.

"Huh?" he said. There was a girl. In the doorway. He hadn't heard it open.

"Hello?" Gabe said. The girl was older than him. Maybe eighteen. She was wearing a black dress with a large red circle on her chest. She was Latina. Long dark hair. Stockings. A small leather bag, cinched closed, on a delicate chain around her waist. Five squirrels scampered around her buckle shoes, looking to her while making hopeful chittering noises. One of the squirrels was so black that it almost looked like a silhouette. The squirrels were soggy from the rain. The girl wasn't. She was entirely dry and entirely frowning at Gabe.

"What a night, eh?" she asked. Her voice was somehow both smooth and raspy, like a singer who'd been singing too loud, too long. "Oh, and hello, Gabe."

"You know my name?" Gabe asked, wary. The girl walked farther inside the café. The squirrels followed, circling her like moons around a planet.

"I know your name," she said, as if his name was obvious. "I know what the moon thinks, and I know how to flirt with rivers, and I know how to calculate the exact amount of surprise in a cat."

"Wow," Gabe said. "That's . . . something."

"I don't always know how to behave, though. I don't want you to think I'm not aware of my faults."

"Who are you?" Gabe asked, trying to keep some distance, but it was hard to do. She kept moving. Not just on her feet, but . . . otherwise. She carried herself like a dancer, every movement full of grace, but at the same time she appeared to be flickering, lost for moments, appearing almost exactly where she had been before, but not quite. A step here and there. Missing. Gone.

"See?" the girl said. "Another of my faults. I forgot to introduce myself. My name is Marsh. I'm one of the others."

"The . . . others?" Gabe asked.

"Think of everyone you know," Marsh said. "And everyone in this city. Everyone in *all* the cities. And outside them, too. Every single person who has ever walked, talked, or breathed. Now, keeping all of those people in mind, I'm one of the others."

"You're not one of . . . everyone?" Gabe asked. "That doesn't make sense."

"Right? I'm *very* good at not making sense. Possibly the best." She paused and then added, "Luther needs to check something. I hope that's okay."

"Luther?" Gabe asked. Things were moving too fast. Too confusing.

"The squirrel on your friend's chest," Marsh said, pointing behind him. Gabe turned and saw the black squirrel was perched on Tradd's chest, gingerly touching a paw to his chin.

"Whoa!" Gabe breathed out. "Why is your squirrel—?" Gabe turned to look back at Marsh, but she walked past him as he turned. She'd been a good ten feet behind him and couldn't have covered the distance in that time. But there she was, striding past.

"The thing is, with the Wardens' helicopters grounded by the storm, I thought you might need help. The doctors, you know. The medics." For some reason she was taking off

Tradd's left shoe. This whole time, ever since Marsh had appeared, Tradd had seemed barely awake, not really paying attention to anything, not even when the squirrel sat on his chest. Marsh unlaced his shoe and placed it on the table next to him, then peeled off his sock and draped it across his leg. Tradd still didn't react.

"What are you doing?" Gabe asked. He reached for Marsh's wrist to pull her away from Tradd, but missed. She simply wasn't quite where he'd expected. She gave him a shrug.

"I heard your friend took a knock to the head," she said. "And, like I mentioned, I knew the doctors couldn't reach you, and I sometimes help them from time to time."

"Who told you about Tradd?" Gabe asked. "And, you help the doctors? Does that mean you're a doctor?"

"The hailstone that hit your friend told me about it. She seemed giddy, if I'm honest. Proud of her aim."

"What? You talk to . . . ? You can talk to *hail*?"

"I'm one of the others, Gabe. We talk to other things. As far as your question about me being a doctor, I'd say I am one, unofficially." She'd taken out a small bottle of toenail polish and was painting Tradd's big toenail black. Gabe was fairly certain he should put a stop to all this.

"Are you with the Wardens?" he asked.

"Unofficially." She was blowing air on Tradd's toenail to dry it.

"Are you . . . a witch?" Gabe wasn't sure if the question was rude.

"Let's say . . . unofficially." She put the toenail polish away in the small bag around her waist.

"You seem to be a lot of things, unofficially," Gabe said.

"*Now* you're starting to understand!" Marsh told him. She put a friendly hand on his shoulder and said, "To be honest, I'm *everything*, unofficially."

CHAPTER 23

Even in the rain, Joon could smell the blood trickling from her forehead. And if *she* could smell it, she knew the vampire could as well. Frozen into position, she wasn't sure what to do. Count Drustan was close. Too close. She'd trained for situations like this, but the reality of having the vampire so near, so hungry, made her feel like she might freeze into ice or simply break down and cry, or—worst of all—allow him to have some blood. There were voices in her head urging her to do just that. To stand before him. To submit. To offer her neck. The voices were whispering, urgent and commanding. The voices weren't hers, however. Joon knew the vampire was putting them inside her mind, but at the same time they *were* there, and they made sense, right? The vampire was hungry. Just a little blood. Just a little.

"No," Joon said, shaking her head as if the voices might fly out of her ears.

"Stay back, Drustan!" Hayden commanded, steadying the tray above her head with one hand while holding out her medallion with the other, using its power to force the vampire—hopefully—back. Count Drustan looked at her with narrowed eyes. A stalemate formed. He could come no closer, not with the medallion blocking his path. But if Hayden moved at all, the vampire could get past her and reach Joon, who was still too shaken by the vampire's intrusion into her mind. It was simply a matter of who was going to blink first, the vampire or Hayden, and Hayden had a feeling she was on the short end of the stick. Maybe if the weather had been less violent, she might have been able to continue her stand, but the hail was battering the tray above her head, her grip failing, with the wind trying to tear the tray free and send it sailing away. She could barely see in the fierce downpour. But none of this seemed to bother Count Drustan. Whatever hail slammed into him only bounced away as if he were a statue, unbothered by the onslaught. He wasn't even blinking.

"Centuries in that coffin," the vampire said. "Alive, but dead. Dead, but alive. Nothing to do but sleep. Nothing to do but wait." His voice was clear, as if the storm was stepping aside to let him have his say.

"Nothing to do but ponder the passing of time," Count Drustan said. His voice was inside Hayden's mind. A direct line to her brain. "Nothing to do but let my senses expand from the underground chamber, listening to centuries slipping past, the tapestries falling, the rats and mice twitching, the breath and the blood of the humans fading, growing ever more distant. My coffin, eternal. Myself, eternal. My hunger, eternal."

Joon was still holding the werewolf's head in her lap, the deepening rainwater rippling around them. The beast's eyes kept fluttering open. Fluttering closed. He stank of wet fur. The blood kept dripping from Joon's forehead. Count Drustan kept watching. Focused.

"Have you ever been hungry, children?" the vampire asked. Joon knew better than to answer, and Hayden was determined not to speak.

"I have known hunger," Joon said. The words came unbidden from her mouth.

"I have been hungry," Hayden said. She hadn't known she was going to say anything. She felt like a puppet, the words forced through her lips. The vampire's mind was overwhelming her as easily as the hail was overwhelming her faltering grip on the tray above her head, and above Joon's head, as well. Without its protection, the hail would batter them. And without the golden medallion she was holding, the vampire would be on them.

"Everything knows hunger," the vampire said with a smile that seemed genuine, although with sadness in his voice. "But nothing knows hunger in the manner of a vampire. It is a fire. It is a hook around our every thought, pulling us closer to the blood. And that hunger grows. Centuries in a coffin. I did not eat. I grew too weak to feel the castle around me. To hear the voices of the night. My world shrunk. Little remained. There was only myself. My coffin. My hunger."

Hayden could feel the pressure of his presence, as strong as the wind.

"Joon Olivia Baker," Count Drustan said, his eyes—his entire being—focused on her forehead. "You have blood on you."

"Do you want some?" she asked. Her question shocked Hayden, who could hear the submission—the offering—in Joon's voice.

"Joon, no!" she shouted. But Joon waved her off.

"Just a little blood," Joon said, her eyes on the vampire. "What could it hurt?"

"Just a little blood," the vampire echoed. "What could it hurt?"

"No! *No!*" Hayden yelled, but the wind swept her words away. Usually, by now—in a Versus battle that was so badly spinning out of control—the Wardens would step in. But the storm had chased them away. The helicopters had been forced to retreat. Perhaps the Wardens were on foot, now. Perhaps they were on their way. But they weren't there at the moment, in the Pedestrian Mall, with the unconscious werewolf and the starving vampire. She and Joon were on their own. And it wasn't going well.

It was time for drastic measures.

Hayden tossed the tray away. The hail, unimpeded,

began pelting her. A few small hailstones she could endure. She had to hope none of the larger ones struck. With both hands free, she could hold her medallion in a much fiercer grip. She could force the vampire away.

"It's okay, Hayden," Joon said, standing up, pushing Hayden's arm—and her medallion—down. "He only wants a little blood."

"Don't do this," Hayden all but begged. "If he starts drinking, he . . . he might not *stop*!"

"Do you promise to stop?" Joon asked the vampire. At her feet, the werewolf was limp in the water, his nose barely above the surface. His dazed eyes were open, but saw little. His body shivered, trying to repair the damage done by his fall and the lightning. His fur was buffeted by the wind, matted by the rain, melted by the terrible heat of the lightning strike. His enormous body quivered whenever the larger hailstones struck. Joon stepped over him, sloshing in the puddle, moving closer to the vampire.

"I cannot promise," Count Drustan told her. "For all my power, I am still under the sway, the *rule*, of centuries of hunger."

"Do your best." Joon shrugged, then wiped blood from her forehead and held out her fingers, shielding the hand from the rain, the blood left unspoiled. Count Drustan's lips pulled back. His fangs were in full view. They were so white. So long. So sharp.

"Joon!" Hayden yelled, trying to pull her back, but once more Joon just shrugged her away. The vampire took the opportunity to sweep closer. He put a hand on Hayden's shoulder, whispered, "I'm sorry," and flung her aside. She skidded along the bricks, tumbling through the puddles to a stop some fifteen feet away. Dazed and bruised, she slumped under the branches of a maple tree, somewhat protected from the worst of the hail. But now there was nothing to protect Joon. Hayden could only watch in horror as the drama played out.

"My blood," Joon told the vampire. "It's what you want, right?"

"It's what I *need*," Count Drustan said. His hands reached for her.

"I'm scared," Joon whispered. She took a step back.

"There's no reason to be scared," the vampire said. The hail kept slamming off his head. He paid no attention to the bombardment. He had eyes only for the blood. His lips curved into a soft, small smile. "Or, perhaps there's a *little* reason to be scared. Or, even perhaps *every* reason." He stepped closer. Joon took another step back. Hayden, watching from afar, was reminded of a cat playing with a mouse, the mouse mesmerized by the presence of the predator and seemingly ignorant of the danger, lost in the fascination.

"I don't know if I should be doing this," Joon said, her voice uncertain. The blood was still seeping from her forehead. She felt weak. The storm was confusing her, as was the vampire's voice in her head.

"What we should do is often different from what must be done," the vampire said. His words carried the weight of centuries. He stepped forward again. Joon, again, stepped back.

"What do you think I should do?" Joon asked in a voice that fluttered in the wind. She remembered how many times in the past she'd asked adults for advice, and how often they'd failed her. She tried not to think of how much older this vampire was than any of the other adults she'd ever met. Over six hundred years. The vampire was an ocean of presence in the middle of the storm. Larger than all the clouds and the lightning.

"I think you should stop moving away," the vampire said. It was almost as if his red eyes were doing the speaking. Joon was transfixed. His voice was so clear in the storm. "I believe you should offer your blood to one who has such need."

"O-okay," Joon whispered. It was so cold. Why was the rain so chilling? Why did the hailstones seem like they were exploding from within her, instead of falling from the sky? There were no answers. There was nothing, in fact, but the vampire. Joon willed her feet to quit stepping back. She kept her eyes on the vampire. He moved forward. His fingers touched her shoulder, then clenched tight. His mouth was so open. His fangs looked colder than the ice falling from the skies.

"Promise me something," Joon said. She tried to step back again, but the vampire's grip was too strong. He was so close she could smell his breath. A sweet, sharp honey. A scent of candle wax. A corridor of stone.

"What would you have me promise?" the vampire asked. His voice was mocking. His words floated in the red laughter of his eyes.

"That you won't be mad for how I'm acting. For how long it took me to offer my blood. For how I made you follow me."

"It took only a handful of seconds," Count Drustan said. His voice was soothing. Alluring. Almost warm. "What is a few ticks of a clock to a vampire? Meaningless."

"I suppose," Joon said. "But . . ." Her voice trailed off.

"But?" the vampire questioned. His teeth were almost on Joon's neck. She could feel the artificial warmth of his life.

"But a few seconds, a minute, is everything to a werewolf," Joon said. "That's why I did this. That's why I led you around with my blood. So that Redd had time to recover." Joon smiled so wide that her own teeth were visible in the night, as bright and as white as the vampire's fangs.

"What?" Count Drustan said in a moment of confusion, looking into Joon's eyes, looking to the blood on her forehead—to the leash that had led him astray from a battle almost won—as he became aware of the werewolf behind him.

CHAPTER 24

The black squirrel glowed briefly, shining light from within before fading back to black.

"Good job, Luther," Marsh said, petting the squirrel on Tradd's chest. Gabe still wasn't sure if he should be letting any of this happen. He was supposed to be protecting Tradd, staying behind in order to make sure Tradd was safe, but instead he was just watching . . . *something* happen. The storm outside echoed the storm Gabe felt in his head. Everything Marsh did felt like a lightning strike, followed by rumbles of uncertain consequence.

"Why did he glow?" he asked Marsh, who had picked up the squirrel and was cradling it in her arms like a baby.

"A medical procedure. You could consider it a healing spell. But it wasn't. Not quite."

"I'm trying to be a warlock," Gabe told her. "That's why

I'm doing all this. Because of my uncle. I'm too late for him, but . . . you know." Something in Marsh's eyes told Gabe that she, in fact, *did* know. It felt like she knew everything. And other things.

"I'm not sure why I told you that," he added.

"I'm never sure why I do anything," Marsh said. "It's nice."

"You said it was a healing spell, right?" Gabe asked. "You're helping Tradd?"

"Of course. That's what I do. And, well, other things."

Gabe was going to question what she meant, but Marsh reached to her chest and the red circle on her black dress. She pried at the edge of the circle and, to Gabe's astonishment, flipped it open like a small, round door. Behind the door was . . . nothing. A cavity. A void. Marsh tucked the black squirrel inside and closed the red door. There was a *click* as it snapped shut. The other squirrels raced out of the café into the storm.

"You're . . . hollow?" Gabe asked, staring at Marsh.

"No. Well, sometimes. Never, really. Not more than a few times a day."

"You haven't made any sense since you came in here," Gabe said.

"Oh, Gabe," Marsh replied. "I haven't been making any sense for a lot longer than that. Now, let's check on your friend." She leaned low over Tradd to give him a kiss on the forehead, and said, "Wake up, Tradd." His eyes were only half-open behind his glasses, but now they opened wider, and while his eyes had appeared dazed, now they had the glint of intelligence.

"Did I pass out?" he asked.

"A little," Gabe said. "But this is Marsh. She's with the Wardens. She's a doctor."

"My name *is* Marsh," the girl said. "But the rest of that was not quite true. Still, if something isn't quite true, it's something else. And that means it's something other. And that is what I am, in truth."

"I'm still feeling a little dizzy," Tradd complained, staring at Marsh, trying to understand her words as she helped him sit up.

"It's a dizzying night," she said. "A werewolf. A vampire. My storm. The purloined muffins. All very chaotic."

"*Your* storm?" Gabe asked.

"Not quite, to be honest." She stopped and sniffed the air, then straightened with a smile and said, "Oh, they're almost here."

"Who?" Tradd asked, putting his shoe back on.

"Them," Marsh said, and she pointed to the door. At first it was nothing but the darkness outside, the rain and wind and the clattering of hailstones on the bricks. But then four squirrels came bounding through the door, chittering in irritation and outrage, all of them carrying a vampire medallion in the manner of several dogs vying for the honor of being the one that retrieved the stick.

"My medallion?" Tradd said, even as the squirrels deposited it at his feet. "Thanks!" The squirrels chittered happily and then scurried over to Marsh and ran around her legs, then out the door into the storm.

"Just in time!" Marsh exclaimed as Tradd picked up his medallion. "That was close."

"Just in time for . . . what?" Gabe asked. Marsh was sniffing the air again.

"They're almost here," she said, just like before.

"The squirrels again?" Tradd asked. But Marsh shook her head.

"Not hardly," she said, just as an inhuman howl came from the darkness outside, followed by what Gabe recognized as Hayden's terrified scream.

CHAPTER 25

Joon leapt back as the werewolf attacked the vampire. The first blow was a brutal slash of the beast's powerful claws across the vampire's back, shredding flesh and cloth, the impact so intense that Count Drustan was flung into the nearby burrito cart. The cart rocked to one side as he crashed to the ground. The vampire bounced once on the bricks and then was suddenly a large black raven taking uncertain flight, staggered by the force of the attack, leaving a trail of feathers as he flapped his wings, striving to gain altitude.

But the werewolf continued his attack. Gone was any semblance of a man. Now it was only the beast, and the beast wanted chaos and savagery. The werewolf rushed forward at astonishing speed, his claws digging into the bricks before he leapt toward the escaping raven. Hayden gasped. Joon, holding a medallion in each hand, cheered. The werewolf, leaping into the air, was just about to clamp his jaws on the raven when . . . there wasn't a raven anymore. Now, perhaps twenty feet in the air, the vampire had become a giant wolf that twisted to avoid the werewolf's attack and clamped his jaws not only around the werewolf's shoulder, but also nearly around his neck. Only a desperate move from the werewolf saved him from losing the fight right there. He managed to forestall the vampire's attack by wedging a fist into the vampiric wolf's jaws, preventing them from closing on his neck. Together, joined by teeth and claw and monstrous rage, the wolf and werewolf tumbled to the ground. Bolts of lightning crashed through the skies and shivered the ground. To Hayden, it seemed like everything was growling, not just the two wolves but the skies as well. The rain still fell, and the alarms still rang, and the massive hailstones pounded everything to tatters. She wanted to take shelter from the storm and the monsters, but the cold and the fear had seeped into her thoughts. The surrounding chaos, the brutality and the sheer speed of everything that was happening, simply pinned her in place.

One moment the vampire was a wolf, and in the next a raven that drove its talons into the back of the werewolf's head, wings flapping madly, savagely pecking at the werewolf's skull. The werewolf roared in outrage and ripped the raven from his neck, flinging the huge black bird at the wall of the Decker Building, but at the last moment the raven simply turned into a mist that flowed out over the bricks, then became a man. A vampire. Count Drustan. He clung to the wall like a spider, scurrying upside down to the ground and then standing like some prince, his clothes in tatters but his smile resolute.

"Such battle," he said. "I have longed for such a contest. To be challenged is to be alive." A shiver rippled through his body as he took his hybrid form, half man and half bat, his powerful wings flapping as he propelled himself to the fight, emitting a high-keening scream that hurt Joon's ears and caused Hayden to clamp her hands over the sides of her head, desperate to block out the agonizing sound. The werewolf staggered, his equilibrium battered by the damaging noise. The man-bat slammed into him and snatched him up in midflight, using his momentum to smash the werewolf into the façade of the Oasis nightclub, with bricks and bones cracking from the powerful impact. Again and again, the vampire slammed the werewolf into the building, with the storm raging all around. One of the werewolf's arms was clearly broken, his hand flexing in feeble fashion, but he managed to twist his other arm behind him, raking his claws through one of the vampire's bat-like wings. Count Drustan hissed in pain, his attack paused long enough for the werewolf to turn the tide of the battle, grabbing the torn bat wing and ripping a part of it free like a paper towel yanked from a roll.

Count Drustan fell to the ground in agony.

The werewolf grabbed the vampire's ankle, using this hold to slap Count Drustan down onto the bricks like a whip. Again and again. Then the vampire changed into a mist, a softly glowing fog that slipped from the werewolf's fingers and drifted to the ground before changing into the vampire, Count Drustan. He crawled forward slowly, sloshing and splashing through the water, apparently unable to stand, coughing and retching. The werewolf hurried forward and kicked him, launching him into the air.

"Oh, dang," Hayden gasped. Not only was the vampire—her hope for keeping her medallion—*losing*, but he was also heading straight at her like a missile. Joon dove for cover, but Hayden was rooted to the spot. The hail thudded against her. Lightning slashed the skies above. The wind shrieked. The vampire was moments from impact. The werewolf howled.

Hayden screamed.

Inside the café, Gabe watched as Marsh—the woman who was not quite a witch—reached out and closed her fingers as if grabbing something, although absolutely nothing could be seen.

"What are you doing?" Tradd asked. Gabe decided he didn't care about whatever strange thing Marsh was doing. He'd just heard Hayden scream, and that was more important.

"I'm moving chess pieces," Marsh told Tradd, and then, with her hand still clenched on nothing, she pulled back, and Hayden fell to the floor at her feet, gasping in shock.

"Hayden?" Gabe asked, as bewildered as she clearly was, but at that moment Count Drustan crashed through the front door in an explosion of glass, smashing into one café table after another, tumbling, and flailing.

Gabe stood in wavering fashion, trying to understand everything that was happening. Where had Hayden come from? What had happened to Count Drustan? And to his own sanity?

"What is—?" he started to question, but then the huge form of the werewolf shouldered him aside, knocking him to the floor as the beast sprinted into the café, took stock of the situation, and howled.

"Vampire," the werewolf said, in a mocking voice, after his long howl filtered away.

"Werewolf," Count Drustan said, mist gathering around him, cats assembling outside the door, peering inside, not daring to enter the café where two monsters were in battle. "You fight well. I admit I thought this would be over quickly. I am pleased to find a worthy adversary."

"I'm impressed you can still stand," growled the werewolf. "I've never met anyone who could avoid my teeth and claws."

"Well, I haven't *entirely* avoided them," the vampire admitted, as the two of them circled each other.

"You're alive," the werewolf chuckled. "That means my aim has not been true." The wind outside raged. The hailstones were a drumbeat to his words.

"Are you okay?" Gabe asked Hayden, helping her to her

feet, keeping his voice down because he didn't want to draw the attention of these two monsters who seemed to fill the café with their presence.

"I don't know what happened," Hayden said, looking around in disbelief. "I was outside. The werewolf hurled Count Drustan at me. I thought he was going to splatter me. But then, I was here?"

"Marsh grabbed you, I think?" Gabe said. "She pulled you out of thin air."

"Marsh?" Hayden asked.

"Her," Gabe said, gesturing to Marsh while keeping an eye on both the werewolf and the vampire. Marsh gave him a little wave and a meaningful smile, although Gabe wasn't quite sure of the meaning.

"Marsh?" Hayden questioned again, a frown wrinkling her lips.

"The witch," Gabe said, again gesturing to the woman in the black dress. "Although she's apparently *not* a witch. She's something else."

"Gabe," Hayden said, looking back and forth between Gabe and where he was pointing. "There's no one there."

"Uh, yes there is? Marsh. She helped Tradd. And brought his medallion back." Gabe looked to Tradd, and Tradd gave a slow nod. Gabe turned back to Hayden and asked, "You don't see her?"

"I don't see *who*?" she asked. Gabe frowned and looked to Marsh, who gave him a meaningful shrug and another meaningful smile, the meanings of which were becoming clear.

"She's standing right there!" Gabe argued, as if stating the same thing louder would make a difference. But Hayden didn't look where he was pointing. She only looked past Gabe, behind him, with wide, frightened eyes.

"*Who's* standing right there?" a voice asked. Gabe shivered. The voice was primal. Grating. It came from behind him. Trying to keep from trembling, and clutching hard on the medallions in his pocket, Gabe turned.

The werewolf was towering over him.

CHAPTER 26

"Who's standing right there?" the werewolf repeated, with a mountain's worth of menace. Gabe slowly slid his werewolf medallion from his pocket.

"Marsh," Gabe answered. "A girl. She's . . . close to being a witch. But not quite."

"You're hallucinating, child," the werewolf said, leaning in closer, his jaws brushing against Gabe's cheek. There was the cold solidity of a fang pressing against his shoulder. "There is nothing there."

"Her name is Marsh," Gabe said. He didn't know why he was insisting.

"There's nothing there, trembling boy," the werewolf said with a snarl Gabe felt all through his bones. "My eyes see in manners where yours fail. And my nose sees in ways that humble my eyes. I can scent the sweat of each person who's been in this café for a week. I could tell you the fabrics of their clothes. I could tell you everything, and I *will* tell you that no one is there. I would know." The longer the werewolf spoke, the more bestial he became, as if each human word were a coin that he was spending, and soon there would be no coins left to spend.

Gabe didn't answer. He couldn't. There were no words with the audacity to leave his throat. His eyes flickered away from the werewolf, to Marsh. She shrugged.

"I am not quite here," she said. "Almost. A little bit. You know, yes, I *do* think I'm here. Let's say that I am. There is a debate, at least. But in the end I am here and I am not. I am, you see, something other." And with that she was gone entirely. Gabe shivered, and he expected the werewolf to—at least in some way—react to Marsh's voice, but the werewolf obviously hadn't heard a word she'd said.

Gabe held up his werewolf medallion.

"It doesn't matter if you saw her or not," he said. "It doesn't matter if you smelled her. What matters is that you're standing too close to me. By the power of this medallion, I—"

"Yes, yes," the werewolf chuckled. "You command me. I get it. Can't you see how *frightened* I am of your little silver trinket?" The werewolf's tone was mocking. "Maybe you'll put that away," he said. "Maybe you'll quit making up stories about people who aren't there. Maybe I'll let you walk out that door." His words were increasingly difficult to understand. There were too many growls in his voice. Too many teeth. The noise of the storm—to Gabe's ears—receded. His awareness of anything but the werewolf diminished. Everything else was a fog.

"Are you mad at me because you're losing the fight against the vampire?" Gabe asked, swallowing. The werewolf's dark eyes went redder around their edges, but Gabe knew he couldn't show weakness. He had to keep his nerve.

"Losing?" the werewolf asked, his voice full of warnings.

"I saw you leaning on the table. I'm noticing your wounds aren't healing as fast as before. I can hear the ache in your voice. You're losing." Everything that Gabe spoke was true. Werewolves heal at phenomenal rates, but even werewolves have limits, and the vampire was breaking them.

"You're weak," Gabe said. He tried to put all his bravery in his voice. He tried not to think about how it wasn't just the werewolf who'd been affected by the battle. He'd also noticed that Count Drustan was having problems. The vampire could no longer entirely control his transformations. His left leg had a constant aura of fog, and his right arm had retained a light smattering of feathers. If Count Drustan was having trouble controlling his transformations, that was a clear sign he'd been pushed to his limits. Vampires heal by changing from one form to another. If Count Drustan was losing that ability, it meant the end of his fight was near.

"Weak?" the werewolf snarled at Gabe. "You think I'm weak?" Gabe felt like he was too close to a flame and that the ground around him was crumbling.

"Yes," he said. "Why else would you be threatening me, a nine-year-old *human*, when there's a *vampire* in this room?"

In that moment, Gabe felt his life was a coin flip. Either the werewolf understood what he was saying, or the creature was too far gone for any words to reach him. One side or the other. A flip of the coin. The medallions didn't seem capable of completely stopping the werewolf, only giving him pause for a brief time. Now, that time was over, and Gabe's life was in the balance. Fifty-fifty. A coin flip.

The vampire, twenty feet away, chuckled.

It was a chuckle that influenced the coin flip.

The werewolf's nostrils flared. His jaw tightened. His gaze switched to Count Drustan, away from Gabe. The muscles of the seven-foot beast rumbled and shivered and tensed and then relaxed. Huge lungs let out a fetid sigh. The werewolf looked back to Gabe.

"Sorry, child," he said, his dark eyes fading to gray. "I've been caught in my own storm, this night. You were brave to stand against my teeth. Foolish, though. Ridiculous, even. But brave." The werewolf turned away. Gabe thought it best to say nothing. Keeping an eye on the werewolf, he walked backward until he was standing with Hayden and Tradd. Together, they held their medallions outward, facing the vampire and the werewolf. Separately, the medallions hadn't done much. Maybe concentrating their force would do the trick.

"Where's Joon?" Tradd asked Hayden. "Didn't she come back with you?"

"I'm not even sure how *I* got here," Hayden answered. "Gabe says it was a witch?" She looked to Gabe for confirmation, still unsure of what had happened to her. She definitely hadn't seen any witch. But a part of her believed Gabe anyway. After all, it had been years since she'd believed the world was required to make sense.

"Hello?" Hayden heard. She looked to the café's broken doorway. Joon was standing outside, battered by rain and hail, but blocked from entry by a veritable swarm of cats. The cats were quickly darting here and there, soggy from the rain, unwilling to step farther out into the storm with its damaging hail, but unable to step any farther into the room. A few rats and pigeons had joined them, seeking shelter from the storm.

"How do I get past them?" Joon asked in a voice nearing a wail, afraid of moving in case she stepped on one of the poor, bedraggled creatures.

"Count Drustan!" Hayden called out. The vampire, his eyes locked on the werewolf, only grunted. He was leaned against a wall, looking like he might collapse if the wall was removed.

"What, Hayden?" he asked, not looking her way.

"Are the cats yours? The pigeons? Are you mentally controlling them? Joon can't get inside."

"I'm busy," the vampire said. "Perhaps you've noticed the werewolf?"

"Just do your mental thing with the cats."

The vampire sighed. In a moment, the cats ceased their pacing and made a path. The pigeons hopped aside. Joon started to walk forward.

"Stop," the werewolf growled at her. Joon stopped. The growl had been persuasive.

"Count Drustan," the werewolf said. "Should we take this outside? A storm makes a more fitting arena than a café, I think."

"I do enjoy this weather," the vampire replied with a smile. Gabe noticed a growing amount of respect between the two monsters. This was the first time the werewolf had used Count Drustan's name, and the first time they'd spoken without any hint of ridicule in their voices.

The vampire turned and strode outside with imperious steps. The werewolf chuckled at how his opponent had arrogantly turned his back on him, but only loped along behind, his left leg somewhat trailing, scuffing over the wet floor of the café. Joon and the cats stepped aside to let the monsters pass. The werewolf knelt down and petted one of the cats, which purred in response, though two others hissed. The rats scurried inside the café the first chance they got, hiding away. The pigeons waddled through the doorway, pecking at things. The werewolf picked up the cat he'd been petting and placed it carefully on a table, inside, away from the broken glass.

"Take care, kitty," the werewolf rumbled, and went outside.

Huddled together in the doorway, Gabe, Hayden, Joon, and Tradd watched the fight between the vampire and the werewolf. Gabe and Hayden held hands. Joon was shivering. Tradd held the frame of his glasses to keep them steady in the fierce wind. Everyone had their medallions at the ready.

Gabe again thought of how he and Hayden hadn't planned to watch the battle along with the other Trainers. He thought of how the storm—the one Marsh had so strangely called *hers*—had forced them all together, even as it kept the Wardens and Crafters away. He thought of how he hadn't planned on meeting a woman who was almost, but not *quite*, a witch.

"He's going to win," Hayden said, gazing out into the storm. "Count Drustan. He's too powerful to stop."

"Care to explain why Redd has been so good at stopping him, then?" Joon asked.

"Getting in a few good punches doesn't win a fight," Gabe argued. "I mean, yeah, he's hurt Count Drustan, but that's only going to make our vampire get serious."

"That's the thing about a werewolf," Tradd said. "They're *always* serious." The four of them lapsed into silence, their throats tired of yelling over the roar of the storm. The hail was finally lessening, at least, down to no more than a smattering of gumball-size hailstones, leaving the area blanketed by hailstones of all sizes. It was *cold* near the hailstones. Joon shivered as she watched the battle play out, hugging her arms to her chest while clutching her medallions.

"You're looking tired," the werewolf told the vampire. The mocking tones had returned.

"I've recently slept for several hundred years," Count Drustan said. "So I feel quite well rested. I feel alive."

"You're not, though."

"There is a debate, yes. Are we here to speak philosophy, then, or for me to prove—once and for all—that werewolves are no match for vampires?"

"This isn't about werewolves versus vampires. This is about me versus you. I care not one strand of fur for any other werewolves. But I will challenge *all* vampires."

"Why?" Count Drustan asked. The question seemed to give the werewolf pause.

"Why?" Redd asked. "Because . . . well, it's obvious. Vampires are . . . oh, I see what you've done. You've forced me into saying that I want to challenge vampires because your kind are so strong that the combat is worthwhile. Fair enough, creature. Fair enough. This fight excites me. I too feel alive."

"For now," the vampire said, and struck. The attack was blindingly swift, like a bolt of lightning given human—or inhuman—form. In the blink of an eye, Count Drustan sped toward the werewolf, a fist pulled back, but at the last second the vampire transformed into his hybrid form, half man and half bat, and used his momentum to flap upward, riding the violent wind with his restored wings, driving a knee into the werewolf's face. The werewolf was sent tumbling across the bricks, splashing through puddles. Coming to a stop in front of the hail-battered pastry cart, he rose groggily to one knee and wiped the water from his eyes, looking up just in time to see the hybrid bat swoop down and grab his arm. The vampire flung the werewolf high into an apartment building, shattering windows with the impact. Instead of bouncing off, the werewolf clung to the building, driving his arm through a window. He yanked a curtain free from inside the window and leapt outward from the wall, slamming into the oncoming vampire and wrapping the curtain around Count Drustan's face, covering his eyes. Together, werewolf and vampire fell to the ground, crashing into the bricks.

"A cheap move," Count Drustan snarled as he stood, ripping the curtain from his face. The heavy cloth was immediately caught in the wind, dancing and twirling like it was alive, soaring up and away, off into the darkness.

"An effective distraction," the werewolf laughed, and tackled the vampire back to the bricks, driving Count Drustan to the ground, clamping his jaws on the vampire's shoulder, ripping and shredding, the bestial form of the werewolf now truly ascendant.

The werewolf bit. Slashed. He shook his immense head back and forth with the vampire clamped in his jaws. Count Drustan bellowed in rage and agony, his hands straining to pry open the werewolf's jaws. He tried to turn into his giant wolf form and strike back, but the transformation was incomplete, a hideous hybrid of wolf and man, a true monstrosity.

"Our werewolf is winning," Joon said. Her words whispered away into the wind, but Hayden heard them and wanted to say something in reply, but there was nothing to be said. Joon was right. The werewolf *was* winning. The vampire, caught in the werewolf's jaws, was being shaken like a rag doll, bitten like a chew toy, terribly injured, lost to the teeth of the beast. Try as he might, Count Drustan couldn't escape the werewolf's jaws. In any battle of biting, werewolves are unmatched.

Except . . .

The vampire quit struggling to escape. In a flickering moment, he once more turned into his human form, and rather than trying to wrench open the werewolf's jaws, Count Drustan bit his opponent.

And drank.

CHAPTER 27

A shrill whine rose from the werewolf's throat, a panicked shriek in the storm. In an instant, it was the werewolf who was trying to escape. He pushed desperately at the vampire, frantically trying to dislodge him, the two monsters rolling on the ground, thrashing across the bricks, splashing through the rainwater. The werewolf let out a series of horrified yelps as his blood began draining, with Count Drustan's jaws locked firmly at the base of his neck. The werewolf was visibly weakening, while the vampire's wounds were healing at an astonishing rate, the slashes and cuts closing, his form no longer leaking mist.

"Heh," Gabe chuckled. Joon and Tradd were silent. Hayden was holding her medallions so tightly that she was cutting off circulation in her fingers, her eyes glued to the savage battle taking place only twenty feet away.

Finally, just when it seemed that all was lost for Redd, the werewolf managed to land a vicious blow atop the vampire's head, and while it *did* serve to sink those terrible fangs even deeper into his shoulder, it also dazed Count Drustan long enough for the werewolf to wrench the vampire free. Gripping the vampire by his throat, Redd slammed Count Drustan to the bricks. A brutal kick then sent the vampire toward a brick wall. He changed into a raven and tried to abort his flight, but only managed to slow his speed before impact. Falling heavily, he was given no time to recover. The werewolf snatched him up and slammed him against the wall several times, until the vampire turned to a mist that flowed from the werewolf's grip and slipped behind him, re-forming into a man and grabbing the werewolf, hoisting him over his head and slamming him to the bricks.

"Oh, wow," Gabe whispered. They were witnessing a battle beyond comprehension. The surrounding storm paled in comparison with this brutality.

Before the werewolf could recover, Count Drustan pinned him face-first to the bricks and knelt on his spine with both hands around the werewolf's chin, pulling back, back, trying to snap the werewolf's neck. The werewolf's muscles went taut as he matched his strength against the vampire, with the vertebrae in his neck and spine creaking, bending, his agony evident, no escape, nothing to do, no way to dislodge the undead creature on his back. Even the werewolf's howl was garbled and broken.

"It's over," Hayden said. There was no way for the werewolf to turn the tide of battle. His terrible claws could not be brought into play. His jaws, useless. There was nothing to be done.

It was at that moment the awning for the Oasis nightclub finally gave way.

Wrenched from its last mooring, the huge awning was swept up by the wind and driven across the Pedestrian Mall. Propelled by the storm, the tattered awning knocked Count Drustan off from his perch on the werewolf's back, carrying him along for nearly twenty feet before the cursing vampire ripped free of the canvas.

"Lucky werewolf," Gabe said. He and Hayden had almost won.

"Whatever," Tradd said, acting as if it was no big deal, but knowing how very close he and Joon had come to losing their medallions.

The vampire strode closer to the werewolf, who was limp on the ground, sprawled over one of the veritable craters the battle had caused, a deep divot in the bricks, filling with water. It was clear that the werewolf could barely move. It seemed like the awning had provided nothing more than a momentary diversion in the vampire's ultimate victory.

"Don't come closer," the werewolf warned, but his voice was weak and his eyes were dull.

"How many times have I heard someone say that?" the vampire mused, walking closer. "I've lost count. But I do know how many times the desperate plea has *worked*. Never. Not once. There is no one who can tell a vampire what to do."

"Don't come closer," Redd repeated, his entire body still limp. "I'm warning you, vampire, do not come closer."

"I've no need to come closer," the vampire said, brushing a hand through the fallen werewolf's fur. "Because I am already here."

The werewolf stared up at him. The two monsters locked eyes.

"I warned you," the werewolf said, and rolled aside to reveal a broken gas main beneath the shattered bricks. The stench of gas filled the area for one moment before the werewolf repeated, "I warned you," and then smashed two fragments of brick together to form a spark.

And the night lit up.

CHAPTER 28

The explosion shattered most of the surrounding windows. For one moment, even the rain stopped, the raindrops blasted back into the skies or evaporated by the fires. Hayden and the others were flung backward, stumbling and falling into the café. A small mushroom cloud rose over the treetops, incinerating what few leaves hadn't been already torn from the branches by the hail. The light was blinding. The heat was agonizing. The sheer noise of the explosion rebounded not only between the buildings, but also within Tradd's skull as he tried to stay on his feet, making sure the others were okay, dragging Joon farther into the café, cats skittering all over between the tables.

In time, it all faded. The fires were reduced to nothing but stray flames licking at the trees for brief moments before the returning rain extinguished them. The broken gas main itself was the only remaining fire, a curved and broken pipe jutting out from a much-enlarged hole in the ground, spitting flame like some bizarre lamp. Steam rose from all around, lending the night an eerie, otherworldly feel. Gabe staggered to his feet and peered outside. The werewolf and the vampire were sprawled thirty feet away from where they'd originally been, tossed by the explosion's incredible force. Neither monster was moving. The werewolf's fur was burned away in huge patches. One of Count Drustan's arms was a broken raven's wing. The rain washed over them, vampire and werewolf both, carrying off the charred remnants of clothing and fur.

"Is everyone okay?" Gabe asked, looking back inside the café.

"M'fine," Hayden mumbled, steadying herself on the cracked glass of the front counter.

"Feels like I'm underwater," Joon said. "My ears are barely working." She was coaxing a gray cat out from beneath a table, where it was huddled with two pigeons. The cat hissed at her, wanting nothing to do with anything or anyone, right now.

"What happened to Redd?" Tradd asked, wiping soot from his glasses. "That vampire?"

"They're down," Gabe said.

"Both of them?" Joon asked, walking with the others as they moved toward the twisted remnants of the front door.

"Both of them," Gabe said, answering even though they were all outside, now, and could see the two monsters themselves. The vampire and the werewolf were barely stirring. A few trembles here and there. Together, the children approached the fallen adversaries carefully, holding out their medallions. A few cats braved the rain to follow along, curious but wary.

"Did you hear that?" Joon asked.

"No," Hayden said. "What are you talking about?"

"Your vampire said something."

"I heard it, too," Gabe said. They were still ten feet away from the monsters.

"They're moving," Tradd said. It was true. Count Drustan slowly rolled over onto his side. The werewolf tried to stand, but failed and collapsed, his face slipping under the water of a deep puddle. Count Drustan noticed and reached over, grabbing a clump of the werewolf's fur and dragging him out of the water. It was all the strength the vampire had left. He collapsed next to the beast, his arm across the werewolf's back.

"He's saying something," Tradd said. "The vampire's saying something."

"Your werewolf, too," Hayden said. Incoherent mumbles were coming from the monsters. Choked words from burned throats, barely audible in the first place, and totally lost in the driving rain and howling wind. Hayden moved closer, passing the gas main's twisted pipe and the warmth of the spewing flames against the chill of the storm.

She knelt next to Count Drustan. He was a wreck. Burned.

Broken. Smoldering. The werewolf was no better. "I can't hear what he's saying," she told the others.

"Be careful," Gabe told her. "He'll be hungry." Hayden nodded and moved back. No matter how far away you are from a starving vampire, you're always too close.

The noises were still coming from the burnt mouths and twisted lips of the vampire and the werewolf. Guttural breathing. Vocal grunts trying to be words. Or... were they? Joon listened closer. The sounds were... they were...

"Oh," she said in realization. "They're not trying to speak."

"They're not?" Gabe asked. "Then, what are they doing?"

"They're *laughing*," Joon said. "They're both... laughing." Hayden turned to look at the two monsters sprawled on the bricks, the vampire and the werewolf at her feet.

"Laughing?" she asked, but even as she questioned it, she realized it was true. They were both laughing. The laughs were horrible, though. Parched and broken and weak. But the two monsters *were* laughing, and the laughs were growing louder, clearer. The two of them were healing. The werewolf's eyes opened. His fur was regrowing. Broken bones mending. The vampire trembled into his raven form, a few feathers out of place. He toppled to one side. His laughter changed into caws. He turned into a wolf and stood on three feet, one leg broken. He turned into a man and was whole. His face was cleansed by the rain. His throat was renewed. The laughter was loud. His smile was enormous.

"You blew me up!" the vampire laughed, using his vast strength to help Redd to his feet, lending the werewolf a shoulder of support. "You set me on *fire*!"

"Your *face*!" the werewolf said. "You should have seen your face when I showed you that gas main! Your eyes went *sooooo* big, and then you screamed!"

"I didn't scream!" the laughing vampire protested. "I mean, maybe? Did I scream?"

"Like a banshee!" the chuckling werewolf replied, sitting down on a badly cracked bench. Count Drustan sat next to him, grinning.

"A banshee's wail, huh? Is that anything like a werewolf when he realizes a vampire is feeding on him?"

"Ha ha! Yes! Almost *exactly*! Seriously, Count Drustan, when I felt your teeth go in, I nearly soiled my fur."

"I can't believe you grabbed my raven form and swatted me against the wall," the vampire said, his eyes filled with mirth.

"*You're* the one who turned into a fog and tried to choke me from inside my own lungs. Fair's fair after that."

"I suppose it does make sense why you blew me up."

"I blew us *both* up. *Not* smart on my part."

"Fun, though," Count Drustan said, looking to the skies. The rain was lessening.

"*Incredibly* fun," Redd mused, wiping water from his face.

"There's your moon," the vampire said, as the moon

made its way from behind the clouds for the first time in an hour.

"So beautiful," the werewolf said in his coarse voice. "That big ol' rock in the sky. So beautiful."

The two of them, werewolf and vampire, sat together in silence, staring at the moon. Standing ten feet away, Joon couldn't believe how quickly the two combatants had—it seemed—become friends. She looked to Hayden and gave a lift of her eyebrow.

"*This* is what it's all about," Hayden said, reading the disbelief in Joon's eyes. "There's a . . . social aspect to the Versus battles. Werewolves and vampires. Ghosts and mummies. All monsters. These creatures rarely get out. Rarely make friends. Humans can break down if we sit alone day after day, cut off from the world, and monsters are no different. What we're really doing is giving monsters a chance to get out of the house, whatever their 'house' might be. It really doesn't matter who wins and who loses."

"Not for them, maybe," Tradd said. "But it matters for us. So, who won? Werewolf or vampire? Which one of us gets to keep our medallions?"

"Oh, I'm not sure," Gabe said. The rain was over, but he didn't feel any less wet.

"Should we ask them?" Hayden said, gesturing to the werewolf and the vampire. "I mean, they're the ones who ultimately decide, right?" Gabe looked to her with a shrug, which Tradd echoed. Joon thought about it and gave a nod. They would let the monsters decide.

"Hey, Count Drustan?" Hayden called out.

"Yes?" the vampire said, looking to her. Cats had begun gathering around the werewolf and the vampire, favoring one monster or another, choosing sides.

"We're really glad you both had fun. But, um, which one of you won the fight?"

"Hmm," the vampire said. He scratched his chin, deep in thought. He looked to the werewolf, but neither of the two monsters had an answer.

"Flip a coin?" Count Drustan asked the werewolf.

"That's ridiculous," Redd said. "So, yeah, let's do it." With that, Count Drustan reached into what little remained of his pants and brought out an ancient gold coin.

"Heads or tails?" he asked the werewolf. Hayden couldn't believe what they were all watching. The fate of her medallion was going to come down to a coin toss?

"Tails," the werewolf said. Count Drustan nodded and then, with a powerful flick of his thumb, sent the coin flipping thirty feet up into the air. Werewolf and vampire watched its ascent. The moon did its best to add to the drama, the gold coin glinting in the moonlight as it rocketed up into the air. Gabe held his breath. Joon didn't blink. Hayden crossed her fingers. Tradd chewed a fingernail. The coin reached its highest point, spinning almost weightless before beginning its return plunge.

Count Drustan caught the coin and slapped it on the back of his hand, then revealed what fate had decided.

"Heads," he said. "I win."

"Aw, *dang!*" the werewolf barked out, then picked up the coin to glare at it, as if he could change its decision with a menacing look.

"Yessss," Hayden said, her eyes shining with satisfaction.

Gabe let out his breath in a long, slow moment of relief.

"Oh no," Joon said, blinking rapidly.

Tradd chewed fiercely on his fingernail.

"Wait a second," the werewolf growled. "*Both* sides of this coin are heads! You cheated!" He held up the coin to show the vampire, outraged. Count Drustan smiled in return, calm in the literal face of a werewolf's rage.

"Not really," the vampire said. "You had your chance to call heads, and didn't."

"Oh, yeah," the werewolf said, calming down. "That's true." He was still studying the gold coin, as if to divine further secrets. "If I would've called heads, I would've won."

"Possibly," Count Drustan said. "But if you had, I might've found a way to cheat."

"Just like a vampire," the werewolf chuckled. "Always finding a way to cheat. You've even cheated death itself." He reached over and gave the vampire an enormous pat on his back.

"I'd *thought* I'd cheated death," Count Drustan said, "until you blew me up. I really can't stress enough how frightening that was."

"An exhilarating moment, I agree," the werewolf said. The two of them stood, looking to the skies for some reason

Hayden couldn't understand. After a few moments, though, she heard the faint sounds of helicopters. The Wardens were returning, now that the storm was fizzling away.

"Looks like our rides are here," Count Drustan said.

"Yeah. Time to go back home." The two monsters, side by side, watched the lights of the helicopters come over the buildings. For long moments, they stood in silence except for the *whupp-whupp* of the helicopters and the shrill insistence of one remaining alarm, ringing out from the Oasis nightclub.

"Here's a thought," the vampire said, turning to the werewolf. "You should come visit me. In my castle. I've some restoration to do. But parts of it are still grand."

"Restoration?" the werewolf replied. "Maybe I could help. I'm pretty handy for a guy with paws, and I've always wanted to work on a castle. Count me in, Count. And, you should come see my forest."

"You have your own forest?"

"He does!" Joon said. "He built a whole forest in a warehouse! It's . . . it was actually quite beautiful."

"Thank you," Redd told Joon, then, turning back to the vampire, said, "If you want to see my castle, come to my forest."

"Mmm," Tradd said, frowning. "Sorry to disagree, but, we saw that shack in your forest. It wasn't exactly what I'd call a castle."

"The *forest* is his castle," Count Drustan said.

"*Exactly*," the werewolf snarled, looking to Tradd, who

squeaked out an apology. Out in the street, just past the Pedestrian Mall, the helicopters were landing.

"I can't wait to get started on your renovation project," the werewolf said as he and the vampire strode toward the waiting helicopters. "You have any rooms big enough for a forest?" Further words were lost to the sounds of the helicopters as the children watched the two monsters walking off. The cats were milling around in confusion, like concertgoers in a parking lot after the show is over.

"Dang," Joon said. "All that for a coin flip. Tradd and I . . . we lose."

"And Hayden and I win," Gabe said, giving Tradd a sympathetic pat on his shoulder.

Together, they walked to the helicopters.

CHAPTER 29

Two weeks later, Tradd was staring at an image of a terrier on his phone. It was his dog, Keeper. A black-and-tan coat. Energetic. Occasionally frenzied. Always wonderful. The photo had been taken just two days before Keeper's disappearance.

"Dummy," Tradd whispered fondly, running a finger over the image, feeling a cold sort of emptiness in his chest.

"Did I ever tell you why we named him 'Keeper'?" he asked Joon. They were in the Crafters Guild where the mummy, Ptahhotep, had run roughshod over the Wardens and badly damaged the building. The floors were now reconstructed. Walls rebuilt. Even the cosmetic work was nearly finished, with Joon helping a crew of painters coat the walls a gleaming shade of white. Tradd was helping the electricians.

"Don't think so," Joon said, although Tradd had told her

the reason behind Keeper's name again and again for the past two weeks. Despite that, she understood he needed to keep telling her. Three years later, he was still feeling the loss of his dog as keenly as she was feeling the much more recent loss of her werewolf medallion.

"We adopted him from a farm," Tradd said, scrolling through more pictures. "There were five puppies. They were all good."

"Of course they were," Joon said. "They were puppies."

"Right. But only one stood out. The best of the five. The best dog of all."

"A keeper," Joon said. She knew the story. She could speak the lines.

"Keeper was the keeper," Tradd said, agreeing, checking a newly installed light switch, turning it on and off. The lights went out. Came back on. Everything was working. The room was almost repaired. Joon felt like *she'd* never be quite repaired, though. The damage of losing her werewolf medallion was enormous. Unfixable. Nothing could be done.

"Lemons," she cursed, feeling the ache of her empty pocket. She no longer knew why she'd volunteered to help at the Crafters Guild. Everything felt useless.

"Lemons," Tradd agreed with her. "What are we swearing about?"

"The obvious," Joon said. The smell of fresh paint was making her dizzy. "We lost our medallions. Count Drustan won on a *coin flip*, of all things. It makes me so mad!"

"We only lost the werewolf medallions," Tradd said.

"We're not done. You think I'm just going to quit looking for Keeper? No way! We're still a part of the Versus." He waved his hand around, showing indisputable truth. Of course they were still a part of the Versus. They were in the building. They'd even helped rebuild it.

"We'll fight again," Tradd said, a rising fire in his words. "We'll get more medallions. We'll win the next fight, and then we'll win two more. We . . . will . . . *win*. You can be a witch, and I'll find my dog. We can do this."

Joon stared at him for several heartbeats. She remembered first meeting him. She remembered him learning about the Versus. In those days, he'd looked so lost. Overwhelmed. Now, standing here in the Crafters Guild, he seemed stronger. More confident. Somehow, he'd lost his werewolf medallion but found his footing. He looked unbreakable. He looked like her friend. Her partner. Her teammate. She could picture three medallions in his hand.

"Lemons," she said. Her curse word.

"Lemons?" Tradd asked.

"Yes. Lemons. I've spent the last two weeks crying when I should have been trying. I felt broken, but now I feel unstoppable. Let's hug!" Tradd's eyes went big as Joon all but flew into him, and her arms wrapped around him. She hugged him tight, with her various paint splatters becoming shared paint smears. After a few heartbeats, Joon stepped back.

"Thanks," she said. "Now, let's go get us more medallions." She walked off toward a door, but stopped and looked back.

"Seriously," she said. "Thanks, Tradd." A blush went across her face.

"It really wasn't anything," Tradd said, determined that he wouldn't blush. But he did.

"It *was* something, though," Joon said. "It really was." She made it to the door, opened it, and looked back again.

"Now, let's go start a fight," she said.

CHAPTER 30

Running her fingers through her dog Flapjack's fur, just behind the cocker spaniel's ears, Hayden looked over to her wall-mounted wish board, the one where she kept her medallions, to see her vampire medallion resting firmly in place. It was *hers*, now. It was final.

Gabe was sprawled on her bedroom floor, reading comics on his phone, wearing a gray T-shirt with an image of Count Chocula, the cereal mascot. Hayden watched Gabe for a bit, then turned back to give Flapjack a final pat. Then, leaning closer to the medallion display board, she touched her vampire medallion with a finger, setting it gently swaying.

This was one of her two bedrooms. She had this one in her dad's house, and another in her mom's house, six miles away. The bedroom in her mom's house was more spacious, but Hayden loved them both equally. Flapjack traveled with her, back and forth, enjoying each move as if exploring an entirely new world every time.

There was a framed illustration on the wall, drawn by Hayden's mom, of a family campout interrupted by a thunderstorm. Heavy wind. Rain. Hail. The drawing now reminded Hayden of the storm during the fight between the monsters, a storm Gabe claimed had been caused, maybe, by Marsh, the Not Quite Witch. A woman Hayden hadn't been able to see. Marsh had called herself one of the others, whatever that meant. Were they an actual group? Not just the others but, the Others? Why was life so full of question marks? Hayden filed the Not Quite Witch and the Others away in her mind for further research. She'd already asked the Wardens about these Mysteries That Needed Solving, but their answers had been evasive at best. That only intrigued Hayden even more.

"You're staring at your vampire medallion again," Gabe said. Flapjack sauntered to Gabe, sniffed his phone, dismissed it, and leapt up onto the bed to nestle himself among the pillows.

"How long did you stare at yours?" Hayden asked.

"Infinity and still counting."

"Doesn't it feel like cheating, the way we won?"

"I mean, maybe if *we* decided on the coin flip, but the monsters did that. There's no rule about *how* they fight. They can use fangs, or flip a coin, or even a pie-eating contest."

"I'm glad it wasn't a pie-eating contest."

"Right?" Gabe said. "We'd have lost. I bet werewolves are the world's best pie-eaters."

"Agreed." Hayden paused and then asked, "What are you reading, and where do you think we can find a sphinx?"

"Those are two widely different questions," Gabe said, drinking from a bottle of grape soda that had already turned his tongue purple.

"It's definitely two questions," Hayden agreed. "Have any answers?"

"Well, I'm reading a comic about a haunted house that literally stalks its victims, with ghouls who slither out at night and drag people back to the house, into the dark well in the basement's dirt floor, and the cold water that waits below."

"Okay, first of all, no. If I'd known what you were reading, I wouldn't have asked. Let's talk about . . . where can we find a sphinx?"

"Egypt. Or Greece. Maybe Iran. I started researching almost the moment that Count Drustan identified our sphinx medallions."

"Me too. Let's compare notes. I have, like, eighty pages."

"That's more than me. I only have seventy-nine." Gabe went for his backpack while Hayden grabbed her notebook. She could hear her dad downstairs talking to someone. Was there a visitor, or just her dad on his phone?

"Have I ever told you what I want?" Hayden asked Gabe, her voice quiet and her eyes moving over the family pictures on her wall.

"You mean when we get three medallions?" Gabe asked. He was on her bed, having an entirely unfair pillow fight with Flapjack. The dog was playfully barking, backing up to avoid Gabe's steadily advancing onslaught.

"Yes," Hayden said. "That."

"Duh," Gabe said. "You want to be a witch. You tell me that all the time."

"That's definitely what I want," Hayden said. "Yep." But in her brain, she was saying, "Oh, my gosh and crackers, Hayden. Tell the boy the *truth*." Her lips formed the words. Her chest heaved as she considered—not for the first time—being honest with Gabe. But the words wouldn't leave her lips. If she kept her hopes of getting her parents back together a secret, then nobody could laugh at her. Nobody could ever say that her wish wouldn't come true.

"Ah, peanuts!" Gabe swore, as the cocker spaniel backed too far off the edge of the bed and toppled over the side, yelping in surprise, clonking his head on the window frame.

"Everything okay in here?" Hayden's dad asked, peeking in the doorway.

"It's just Flapjack," Hayden said. "He—" That was as far as she got before the cocker spaniel leapt up onto the bed and started barking at the pillows. Gabe sat there innocently, looking to Hayden's dad.

"Ah, okay." Hayden's dad grinned. "Just the usual weirdness from weirdos. Anyway, you both have a visitor." He stepped back as Quinn Obermark walked into the room. The Warden had a large medallion-shaped purse slung over her shoulder. Despite her bumblebee-shaped barrette, her hair was messy. It was windy outside.

"Quinn?" Hayden gasped, eyes wide. She hadn't expected any visits. Had something gone wrong?

"She's a Warden," her dad said, seeming lost, gesturing to Quinn. "The one you told me about."

"Yes, Dad. I know. Because . . . I'm the one who told you?"

"Yep, yep," her dad said as he headed for the door. "Listen, I'll be downstairs. Tell me about it later." Flapjack, predictably, had decided Quinn was his new best friend, barking happily as he raced around her before leaping back up onto the bed and rolling around on the pillows.

"Your dog is . . . not sedate," Quinn said.

"Flapjack lives life, uh, big," Hayden said. "So, it's great to see you and all, but why?"

"Right to the point, eh?" Quinn said, digging in her purse. "Well, don't worry, it's nothing bad. Sorry to arrive unannounced, but I brought you something."

"Oh?" Hayden said. "For me?"

"For both of you. Here." She brought out a dusty, ancient-looking jar from her purse, made of clay with painted hieroglyphics. It had a removable lid shaped like a cat's head. She handed it to Gabe.

"Yours," she said. "If you want it. Yours and Hayden's."

"Huh?" he said. "It looks old. What are all these symbols? Hieroglyphics?"

"Oh, my gosh and crackers!" Hayden blurted, staring closer at the jar. "You're *kidding* me!"

"What?" Gabe asked, wondering why she was suddenly so excited.

"There!" she said, tapping on the side of the strange jar. "Look!"

Gabe looked where she was pointing, but it didn't mean anything to him. Just more painted symbols.

"Ptahhotep!" Hayden blurted. She turned to Quinn and said, "Are you seriously *serious*?"

"You helped us out so much," Quinn said with a pleased smile. "The Board of Wardens all voted and decided this was the best course of action."

"What's happening here?" Gabe asked, looking between Hayden and Quinn. On the bed, Flapjack was barking, caught up in Hayden's excitement.

"He obviously liked you," Quinn said, talking to Hayden. "And you obviously knew what you were doing, so, yes, it's yours. *If* you can earn it, that is."

"Of course!" Hayden said, all but dancing. "This is so great!" She swept up Flapjack and gave him a clenching hug and a gushing kiss on his nose. She even almost kissed Gabe. *That* would have been embarrassing.

"*What's* so great?" Gabe asked.

"Open the jar," Hayden said, with the impish smile of someone with a secret they're eager to share.

"Open it?" he asked, looking first to Hayden, who gave him an impatient "get on with it" roll of her eyes, and then to Quinn, who nodded.

So he opened the jar. And, inside . . .

"Oh, wow," he whispered. His hands began trembling.

"Ptahhotep," Hayden gushed. "You understand?"

"I . . . yes," Gabe said, reaching inside the jar to where there were two alabaster medallions on silver chains. The identical medallions had a "V" on one side, and on the other they had the image of a mummy's head, tiny red jasper gemstones serving as the mummy's eyes, the carvings so fine that the individual tatters of the mummy's wrappings could be distinguished.

"So, do the two of you want a mummy?" Quinn asked.

"Do. We. Want. A. Mummy?" Gabe said. The words came out slow. Singular. "Of course!" he added.

"Yes, please!" Hayden gushed out. Flapjack, sensing the mood, leapt from the bed and started running in circles again. Hayden felt like running around with him.

She had a mummy.

EPILOGUE

Amos Funada tapped on the hallway's badly faded wallpaper. The house, situated on the outskirts of Paranaguá, Brazil, was dilapidated. From his research, Amos knew nobody had lived in the house for almost forty years, but he'd also discovered how that didn't mean the house was uninhabited.

"Anything?" Lilly Concannon asked, a few feet down the hall, straightening a framed painting of a boy holding an ear of corn. The wire holding the painting broke when she adjusted it, so she let out a sigh and set the painting on the floor, leaned against the wall. She tapped on the nail that had held the painting and thought of the people who'd lived here, so long in the past. Who had driven that nail into the wall? Who had laughed in this hallway? And who still made this house their home, now, so long after the living were gone?

Lilly was twelve years old, with red hair that curled around her freckled ears, and occasionally—irritatingly—over her deeply freckled face. She had pronounced eyebrows, amber eyes, and two front teeth that other people claimed were attractive, though she felt made her look like a confused chipmunk.

"Nothing," Amos said, still rapping his knuckles on the walls. "No hollow sounds. For an abandoned house like this, it's surprisingly solid."

"I'm sure there's a secret room here somewhere," Lilly said. "We just have to find it." She wasn't impatient. The two of them had spent months researching this house, a week traveling to Paranaguá, and a full day to get to this house. It had only been a half hour ago when she and Amos had used a crowbar to pry off the boards blocking the front door, and they'd entered into the eerie dust and decay. Thirty minutes was far too soon to be impatient, now that they were so close to their goal.

Lilly looked around the house. It had obviously been abandoned in a rush. There was furniture in the living room. Potted plants long since dead. Paintings of horses, pictures of relatives and friends, a framed piece of child's art, with four people standing together. Despite the layers of dust, the smell of the house was surprisingly clean, like a winter's morning. There were two stories, including the attic. No other houses within a block. The yard was overgrown. A birch tree had fallen across the back porch, crushing the tin roof and a small wading pool.

"Do you hear whispers?" Lilly asked Amos. "I hear something like whispers."

"Whispers?" Amos asked. Like Lilly, he was twelve years old. Just under five feet tall, with a mop of dark hair so thick it resembled a helmet. Black pants currently covered in dust. A red shirt.

"Like, itchy whispers," Lilly said, adding a shrug to let Amos know she was fully aware of how poorly she was describing the noise.

"From where?" Amos asked. That was one of the things Lilly liked about him. He always believed her. From the day they'd become partners, he never thought she was making things up. He knew there were beings in this world that couldn't be seen or heard or sensed in any manner, but that existed nonetheless. And he knew that, sometimes, these hidden creatures revealed themselves to one person, but not another. Looking for explanations was useless.

"This way?" she said, pointing to the kitchen doorway. The maybe-whispers kept shifting, coming from one direction for a moment, another direction in the next. But they were loudest—Lilly thought—from the kitchen.

Together, they moved down the hallway. There was a decorative table showcasing a wide variety of old glass medicine bottles. Lilly was drawn to the collection. Who had collected them, their faces lighting up when discovering a new treasure? She reached out to pick one up, but when her hand neared the glass bottles, the whispers flared. She moved her hand back. The whispers receded. She moved her hand forward. The whispers flared again.

"What are you doing?" Amos asked.

"Nothing," Lilly answered. It was too weird to explain. She moved on down the hallway, feeling like a hunting dog guiding a hunter, aware of something that the hunter couldn't sense. The whispers were coming from the kitchen. She was sure of it now.

"There's less dust," Amos said.

"What?"

"Less dust," Amos said, pointing to the floor. Lilly looked and it was true. The closer to the kitchen, the less dust on the floors and walls.

"What's *this*?" Amos questioned. He was looking at . . . smoke? Or . . . shadows? Lilly couldn't be sure. There were lines of watery darkness running down the walls, as if the walls were leaking. Lilly could even hear the trickling noises, but there was no water, only the dark flowing lines of smoke. Amos touched one wavering line. The darkness flowed around his finger. Sounds began all around them. A door slamming. The shriek of car brakes. A cough. Somebody humming. Lilly could see her breath in the hall, although it was nearly eighty degrees outside. She heard somebody run past them, though there was nobody to be seen.

"Are you hearing all this?" she asked Amos. His eyes were wide, and he was looking all around.

"The dog barking?" he asked.

"I don't hear that," Lilly said. The lines of smoke kept flowing. Lilly heard a girl's voice saying, "I don't want to go. Why is she sick? I don't want to go." The whispering came from above. From below. From all around.

"The barking is so loud," Amos said.

"I don't hear it," Lilly told him. "I'm hearing other things." Together, they moved on, walking to the kitchen. The doorway was only five feet away. Lilly took a deep breath, inhaling cold, chilling air. They turned into the doorway and looked into the kitchen.

It was empty. Hastily abandoned, like the rest of the house. There were still dishes in the sink. An open cupboard full of dishes. A dining table with a half-eaten, now rotten meal, an accumulation of mail, and a half-full laundry basket. A shelf displaying more decorative glass bottles. Hand-painted flowers on the plaster walls. Roses and orchids and sunflowers.

"Nobody," Lilly said. But the noises were everywhere. Wind chimes. The tinkling of a fork on a plate. A chair scraped along the floor, although none of the chairs were moving.

"Nobody," Amos agreed, the two of them standing in the kitchen doorway, looking inside, barely breathing, just as a hidden door opened in the wall beside them.

The secret door slid back. A cascade of dust. And a ghost came out.

She was largely transparent. Clouds of dust that were sometimes nothing, but at times formed into the face of a young woman in her twenties. No colors. Only dust. Wide eyes. An open mouth. She was a whirl in the air. A floating corpse made of dust. So cold. Always whispering. Lilly could understand her words, now.

"House," the ghost said. "Visitors. Stay? Stay forever?" Her hands of dust reached out. The fingers were far too long. The cold was intense. The watery lines of black shadows began flowing down all the walls, from all around.

"We're not going to stay," Lilly told the ghost, choking down a scream.

"You're not going to stay, either," Amos added. His skin was goose-bumped. He couldn't stop shivering.

"You're going to leave, with us," Lilly said, holding up her glass medallion with its image of a ghost. Amos brought out his own medallion, holding it out.

"We want you to fight a mummy," he said.

ACKNOWLEDGMENTS

Writing a book is a sort of . . . solo group effort, if that makes sense. Yeah, the writer is 100 percent in charge of driving (and even designing/creating) the car, but the author doesn't REALLY arrive at their destination without a LOT of people along the way giving directions and keeping them on the best roads. It was most definitely that way for me. Huge thanks to Jenny Bent, at the Bent Agency, for putting a full tank of gas in my car. And Alex Borbolla at Bloomsbury helped SO much with shaving off the extraneous parts of the novel and helping me heighten the characters and the story. (I'm done with the "car journey" analogy, now: Alex would want me to Get On With Things.) Copyeditor Jeff Curry deserves ample credit, too, although he barely caught over four thousand mistakes. The whole gang at Bloomsbury have been incredibly helpful, and the tribe at Bent have been angels.

Massive thanks to cover artist Doug Holgate for capturing not only the characters but the feel of the series. Looking back, I remember the EXHAUSTIVE search for a cover artist. The seemingly ETERNAL process began with Alex sending Doug's art along as a possibility, and I said he'd be fantastic, and then he was aboard. Oof! Publishing is HARD. The search must have taken, oh, five minutes. Sometimes the first pitch is the best, and ya gotta swing that bat!

Thanks to Colleen Coover, my wife and inspiration and muse and so forth. Everything I do is for her, in one way, although she never reads a single thing I write because she's afraid she wouldn't like it, and then what would she do? So, since she won't read this, honey, I actually did eat those last slices of pizza.

Steve Lieber, Ben Fisher, Jeff Parker, you guys all rock. Adam Knave, Chris Roberson, Brandon Scifert, you also rock. I think it's Big Time important to have a group of fellow creatives that you can get together with and talk about your arts, or NOT talk about them, but still feel like you're around people who understand you. Writing, in a way, is all about making people understand your characters and your story, so it helps to have that feeling in your heart.

To every barista who gave me coffee, thank you. To everyone who let me pet their dogs, thank you. You made this book possible.